GHOST GIRL

ALLY MALINENKO

KATHERINE TEGEN BOOKS
An Imprint of HarperCollins Publishers

Katherine Tegen Books is an imprint of HarperCollins Publishers.

Ghost Girl
Copyright © 2021 by Ally Malinenko
All rights reserved. Printed in the United States of America.
No part of this book may be used or reproduced in any manner
whatsoever without written permission except in the case of
brief quotations embodied in critical articles and reviews. For
information address HarperCollins Children's Books, a division of
HarperCollins Publishers, 195 Broadway, New York, NY 10007.
www.harpercollinschildrens.com

ISBN 978-0-06-304460-9

Typography by Carla Weise
21 22 23 24 25   PC/LSCH   10 9 8 7 6 5 4 3 2 1
❖
First Edition

FOR JAY.

WHO ALWAYS BELIEVED I COULD DO ANYTHING—

EVEN THIS.

THE STORM THAT TORE THROUGH KNOBB'S FERRY WAS UNLIKE ANY
that Zee Puckett had ever seen in all her eleven years.
The wind lashed at the tree branches that knocked
against her windows. The trunks groaned, straining in
the wind that howled up the road. The sky exploded in
lightning, so much that it seemed to be coming from
one hundred different clouds, and then seconds later
a clap of thunder would shake the whole house. It felt
like a bad dream. Zee sat by her bedroom window all
night long, blanket wrapped around her, watching the
streets turn into rivers, mud churning and sloshing up
against parked cars. The whole thing was downright
witchy, and Zee delighted in every second of it.

You see, nothing exciting ever happened in Knobb's Ferry. It was a small town nestled in the mountains. No one spectacular had ever come from there, and nothing spectacular had ever happened. It was the sort of place that people called "sleepy," but to Zee it was more than sleepy. It was comatose. Which was what made this storm the most exciting thing that had happened in a very long time. The second most exciting thing was when Catherine Cooke discovered she had a peanut allergy at the Summer Fair and her face got all swollen and they had to call an ambulance. But that was nothing compared to this storm. Zee reasoned that with the streets being nothing but mud-soaked ruins, at least one building in town had certainly washed away.

She prayed it was the school.

Just north of Knobb's Ferry was a much bigger town, famous for being the home of the classic ghost story about a headless horseman and the knock-kneed Ichabod Crane. Lots of folks came to visit that town. Sometimes they stopped at Knobb's Ferry to get gas on the way, or for a slice of pie at the diner, but they always left after that. That seemed to be the thing about Knobb's Ferry. It wasn't the sort of place you stuck with. It was the sort of place you moved on from. In fact, Zee's parents had also moved on—but in a much different way. Now it was just Zee and her sister, Abigail, who was ten years older than her. Abby worked in the diner, and Zee spent a lot of time there practicing her storytelling skills on the people who passed through. Sometimes if they liked the tale enough, they bought her a slice of pie too. It seemed that was the most you could get out of Knobb's Ferry, a one-horse town with nothing but a pizza shop, a library, one traffic light, and a cemetery. The cemetery was the only part Zee cared about. It was old and huge and macabre—a new word she learned that meant ghastly and ghoulish. Just like Zee's favorite stories.

The morning after the storm, the street awash with mud and tree branches, Zee bounded down the steps from her bedroom into the kitchen, where her sister was putting together lunch. The house was an old creaky thing, drafty in the winter and stifling in the summer, even with all the windows thrown open. Only fall and spring ever felt remotely comfortable.

"No school today," Zee said cheerfully. "They announced it on the radio!"

"Yes, I know."

"And you're not happy about it."

"No, because even though you don't have school, I still have work. Figures the diner is the only restaurant

3

in town with its own generator," Abby said with a sigh as she rummaged through the fridge. She adjusted her long black hair in a ponytail. Zee thought that her sister, Abby, was super pretty, but as she always told Zee, she was too busy holding things together to date. Or to care about how she looked. The biggest difference between the girls was that while Abby had coal-black hair, Zee had the opposite. The exact opposite, in fact. Zee's hair was white. She was a towhead, or flaxen-haired. Most kids Zee knew that had hair like hers grew out of it by the time they started school. Zee's hair, on the other hand, seemed to double down and stay white year after year. Having bone-white hair didn't help at school, where the other kids were quick to jump at any opportunity to tease her.

"And," Abby said, throwing some Tupperware in a plastic bag, "if I have work, that means you're coming to the diner."

All the excitement fizzled out of Zee like a wet firecracker. "No, Abby, please."

"You can't stay here."

"I can! I promise. I won't go anywhere or do anything. I'll stay here, reading books all day, and when you get home, I'll have dinner made."

Abby made a face. Hand on her hip, she said, "You never make dinner."

"I will, though!" Zee said with enthusiasm. "I can make spaghetti . . . or cereal or . . . something." Truth was Zee had never even boiled water, but how hard could it be? You just stick it in a pot, right?

"Get your shoes on. I'm going to be late."

"Abby, please. I'm old enough to stay home."

But Abby ignored her, moving though the cluttered, in-desperate-need-of-a-cleaning house. With it being just the two of them, and Abby working double shifts at the diner, things like cleaning took a back seat, even though technically it was Zee's job. But Zee's theory on cleaning was simple: What's the point? It's just going to get dirty again so you might as well leave it.

As Abby dug around looking for her keys, swearing the whole time that they were on the coffee table last night, Zee followed her, arguing about why she should be able to stay home. Truth be told, it was a rather convincing list. She was already on her ninth point when Abby, moving a pile of clean but unfolded laundry from the couch to the love seat, yelled in frustration, "Zera Delilah Puckett, get your shoes on right NOW!"

It took everything Zee had not to respond. She kept her face as still as possible even though underneath she was fuming. Having white hair was an inconvenience in sixth grade. But a nickname? A nickname was the kind of thing kids at school latched on to—something you couldn't run from, taunting jeers in the hallways. Which was why Zee *hated* her full name, and her sister knew that. As the kids at school had proved, it was far too easy to turn Zera into Zero.

"Abigail," Zee said calmly. "I would like to stay home. I have no school today, and I'm old enough to take care of myself. You already made me lunch." She pointed at the brown paper sack on the kitchen table. "I have plenty of books to read. I will not leave the house, and I will lock the door after you. I've been really good lately."

This, Zee realized, was debatable, but she continued, "And I think I deserve this opportunity to prove myself." She stood with her hands behind her back, balanced on the tips of her toes as if looking taller would translate into being more responsible. But Abby didn't notice—she continued to wander around the house looking for her keys.

"They were right here before," she muttered. She glanced up at the clock on the wall. "I'm going to be late. Again."

Since Zee knew there was nothing that Abby hated more than being late, she counted slowly in her head. It was crucial to get the timing right. As she got to twenty and heard Abby groan and flip over a couch cushion, she knew she was at that sweet spot.

"Abby," Zee said as innocently as possible.

Her sister ignored her, continuing to send the entire living room into chaos in her hunt for those keys.

"Abby?"

"They were right here, five minutes ago. This is ridiculous!"

"Abby?"

"WHAT?" Abby said fiercely. She was frazzled and late and, Zee could see, not in the mood for any of this. Which, of course, made her ripe for the emotional picking.

"I found your keys," Zee said, holding them out in her hand. She debated offering a small shy smile but decided that would be too much.

"You . . ." Abby's shoulder slumped as the anger seeped out of her. "Thank you, Zee."

Zee looked down at the ground, trying as hard as possible to be adorable.

Her sister sighed. "You promise not to leave?"

Zee perked up. "I promise."

"If I call, you'll pick up?"

"Unless I'm in the bathroom, for sure."

"Don't turn on the stove," Abigail said, heading

toward the door. Zee followed, nodding, the giddiness of a whole day ahead of her tingling through her bones. "Don't open the door for strangers."

"Of course not. Though your chances of being murdered by someone you know are far greater."

"You open that door for anyone and *I'll* murder you."

"Exactly my point."

When she reached the door, Abby turned and looked at Zee with doubtful eyes. Zee straightened up. If she could have manufactured a briefcase and suit she would have. "Don't make me regret this."

"Never," Zee said, throwing her arms around her sister. She wagered this might have been a touch too far, but Abby relaxed into her hug and she knew the deal was done.

"I love you," Abby said, kissing the top of her head.

"I love you more."

Abby smiled. It was what their father always said. What was amazing was that Abby still failed to realize that it only came out of Zee's mouth as a way to twist her sister's emotions into delicate little knots.

"Lock this door," Abby said on her way out.

"Will do. See you for dinner."

When the door shut, Zee got up on tiptoes and peeked through the peephole and watched her sister descend the front steps, navigate the river of dried-up mud, and get in the car. It took three attempts, but finally the old thing started and Abby backed down the drive and turned onto Hickory Lane. Once she was far enough from the house, Zee ran upstairs, put on her jeans, her favorite T-shirt, and her hoodie and then crammed her feet into her boots. She threw the lunch her sister made her into her backpack, and faster than you can say "boo," she was out the door and on her way to Elijah's house.

ELIJAH WATSON TURNER—NEVER EVER ELI—WAS ZEE'S BEST AND ONLY friend. Elijah moved to Knobb's Ferry when they were in the second grade, and the two of them became thick as thieves. It was a symbiotic relationship—they each brought what the other needed. Zee needed someone to listen to all her stories. Elijah needed to hear them, even if he sometimes listened with his hands over his ears.

Her boots already muddy, she approached Elijah's house on the corner. It was the exact same layout as her own house, with the exception of one extra step leading downstairs, a fact that quite literally tripped Zee up when they were younger.

"Elijah," Zee called, banging on the door. "You home?"

When the door opened, Elijah stood there— pudgy-faced, sleepy-eyed, his hair faded up the sides until it puffed out into an Afro. He yawned. "What are you doing here, Zee?"

"What do you mean? We have no school today! Let's go."

"I hardly slept last night because of that storm."

"Same! Wasn't it great? It was like something out of a horror story. Now, come on, get your boots on. We're going to the cemetery."

"The cemetery? Why?"

Zee leaned in until her nose was pressed flat against the mesh of the screen door and with a smile said, "Because this storm probably pulled half the coffins out of the ground. Let's go!" She bounded down the steps without waiting for a reply.

"I don't know." Elijah said. "That sounds . . ."

"It sounds amazing," Zee said over her shoulder. "Come on, we have the whole day!"

Elijah chewed his lip and Zee gave him her most confident smile. She knew he would give in. He always did.

"Um . . . okay, let me see," Elijah said, disappearing from the door. Within a few minutes, Zee could hear the deep baritone of Elijah's father's voice. She sighed. How many times did she have to tell him that it's easier to ask for forgiveness than permission? When Elijah did appear, he had the same nervous expression he always wore after speaking to his father, but he had his coat on. They were silent as he followed her down his front porch.

"You okay?" Zee asked as they turned off his street.

"Fine."

Zee knew that tone and knew it was best to let it go. There was always tension between Elijah and his father. Most of it was because Elijah was a little on the bigger side and hated sports, while his father used to be a football player and still had the body to prove it—the rest, Zee assumed, was probably Elijah's friendship with her. Elijah's father wasn't a fan of Zee, mostly because she had a talent for landing in the principal's office. There was no point in talking about either of those things now, though, so instead Zee told him a new story she'd been working on as they sloshed through the mud to the cemetery.

"This rich old baron was hosting a party at his big mansion on the hill. One of his guests asked him if he had ever seen a ghost. While some of the other guests laughed, the old man turned serious. 'Seen a ghost,' he asked, putting a thoughtful hand to his chin. 'Of course I have.' The other men in the room went silent," Zee said, picking her way around a downed tree, Elijah just behind her. "Dead silent."

"So," Zee continued, "the old baron told this story. 'When I was a young man at college,' he said, 'I had a terrible case of insomnia. For what seemed like weeks on end, I couldn't sleep. During this time, I would lie awake at night and *see* things. Shadows and light would come together to form strange illusions. Tricks of the eye. But one night it was more than that. One evening, as I read by the fire, I saw in the shadows a pair of eyes. Bulging, veiny, bloodshot eyes with drooping lids. I closed my own eyes in horror, but no matter what I did, the eyes stared back at me. There was no face, mind you. Not one that I could see. Nothing but those rheumy eyes.'"

"Nice vocabulary word," Elijah said.

"Right? It's when eyes are all slimy. Like with mucus."

"Yes, I know," Elijah said, causing Zee to scowl as they neared the cemetery. She hated how Elijah always liked to subtly bring up how he was in all the advanced classes.

"So the old man says, 'I couldn't get away from those eyes. I moved. I changed jobs. I did everything I could, but those eyes just followed me each night.'

'What did you do?' one of the guests asked. 'Nothing,' the old baron said. 'One day it just stopped. I put it out of my mind, you see. In fact I haven't thought about those old eyes in quite some time.' The baron got up and crossed the room to the fireplace. Above it was a large mirror, and when he looked up, he screamed in terror!"

At this point Zee screamed so loud that Elijah nearly leaped out of his skin.

"What is *wrong* with you?" he said, catching his breath.

"The old man looked in the mirror and said, 'The eyes! They're back!' And fell over dead from a heart attack."

Elijah made a face. "I don't get it."

Zee sighed, her shoulders slumping. "They were his *own* eyes. That's what he saw all those years ago. His own soon-to-be-a-dead-man's eyes."

"Oh!" Elijah said. "That was a good one, Zee, but I think it needs a little more work. You need to make it obvious that they were the same eyes. I don't think listeners would immediately think he was haunting himself. But you should work on this one. It's got potential."

Zee smiled. This was why she liked trying her stories out on Elijah. He always made them better.

They slipped through the wrought-iron gates of the cemetery and picked their way through the mud. There were a few downed trees, as well as toppled-over headstones. They tried to pick a few up, but they were far too heavy. The steep hillside was now just a mud slide, which they attempted to coast down like skiers, but their boots got stuck. Much to Zee's disappointment there wasn't one exhumed coffin. They ate their lunch on one of the stone benches.

"Remember when we used to play hide-and-seek here?" Zee asked.

"Sure," Elijah said, watching a flock of birds cross the sky. "That was when we were kids."

"Oh, I know," Zee said as breezily as possible. Sometimes it felt like time was going too fast. Soon they would be teenagers. And while Zee sometimes looked forward to that, many other times she missed things from her childhood. How much easier everything was back when it was just her and Elijah playing games as third graders. Now that they were in sixth grade, everything seemed like it had gotten more complicated.

"But . . ." She hesitated. ". . . it was still fun."

"Are you serious, Zee?" Elijah said with an eye roll.

"What? Is there someone here to judge you? I'm

just saying. It was fun when we could still do that."

Elijah smiled, and before she could think, he sprang up, smacked her arm, and yelled, "You're it," and took off down the hillside.

Zee cursed under her breath and then started counting, unable to stop the smile on her face.

When she got to ten, she screeched, "I'm gonna find you, Elijah Watson Turner!" She searched everywhere, jumping out and yelling "boo" when she rounded the first mausoleum—but Elijah was nowhere to be found. She trotted around the pond at the center of the graveyard and peeked behind all the big wide tree trunks. It wasn't until she got to the newer section of the cemetery that she stopped. The gate was open. He must have gone in there.

Go, Zee told herself. But her feet wouldn't move. Everything felt locked and rigid and suddenly it was hard to breathe. A flock of birds burst out of a nearby tree, and Zee jumped. *Stop being so scared,* she told herself. *You're not afraid of anything.*

This was true for the most part. Zee wasn't scared of ghost stories; in fact, they were her favorite. She wasn't scared of spiders or monsters or the dark or even dying. But no matter what she did, she couldn't get her feet to move one step forward into the new part of the cemetery. Next to the gate was a large weeping willow tree, and its limbs swayed gently, as if daring her to go in.

A cold wind whipped up, sending leaves across the path in front of her. The sun moved behind a storm cloud, suddenly covering the cemetery in shadows. Something inside her turned cold. She spun around, sure someone was watching her. Her fingertips started to tingle as her eyes bounced from shadow to shadow, stone to stone. Her heart was in her stomach. Something felt . . . wrong.

Off.

"Elijah?" she said softly. "Is that you?"

There was a large black shadow that seemed to move from one gravestone to the next, creeping closer to her. It looked like a dark hunched thing, crawling on all fours across the grass inching closer to her. She told herself it was just Elijah, but she knew that Elijah didn't move like that. No *human* moved like that.

The shadow dipped behind a large headstone with a solemn angel carved on top and then seemed to vanish before appearing again behind another large cross, growing and oozing until the shadow had doubled, now twice the size of the cross.

As it got closer, the shadow morphed into a thing with four legs, a large humped back, shaggy ragged fur, a sloping snout. It was bigger than any dog she'd ever seen in her life, and it moved with the grace and confidence of a wolf. As it crept closer, ducking in and out of the shadows, Zee could swear it was watching her. *Just a stray*, she told herself. *Someone's lost dog.*

The creature crept closer, coming out of the shadows. It stopped and lifted its huge head. She could see its fangs jutting out of its snout, lips curled back in a snarl. When it looked at her, her heart froze solid in her chest.

She blinked, but nothing changed.

The dog . . . hound . . . *wolf* had bloodred eyes— not just the pupil, but actual streaks of blood running from its eyes, down its ragged fur, staining its jutting teeth. It stood there still as a statue, those red eyes fixed on her, watching as if daring her to make a move.

As if daring her to even try to run.

When her scream finally clawed its way up her throat, it didn't take long for Elijah to come running out of the new section of the cemetery.

"What happened?" he asked. Zee wrenched her eyes off the hound and turned to her friend. "Why were you screaming like that?"

Zee looked back to where the dog had been, but it was gone.

"I saw . . ."

"What did you see?"

As her heart banged around in her chest, the word she wanted was right on her tongue.

A demon. She saw a demon.

But instead she said, "A . . . dog."

Elijah started to laugh. "A dog got you screaming like a baby?"

"Shut up, Elijah," Zee said, squeezing her hands so he wouldn't notice how they shook.

"Has the Great Unspookable Zee finally found her terror?" He was doubled over at this point. "Scared of a *dog*!"

"Listen to me," Zee said. "It wasn't a normal dog. It was huge. Like a wolf. And it had . . ." She swallowed, knowing how this was going to sound. But she'd seen it with her own two eyes. "It had red eyes. Bleeding red eyes."

Elijah smiled. "Is this another one of your stories?"

"It's not a story, Elijah. I really saw it."

"Sure," he said with a smirk. "I have to get home. My dad is going to kill me. Let's cut through the new section and take the other gate down by Main Street." He headed toward the willow tree.

"Wait, no," Zee said. The thought of stepping one foot past that willow tree was too much for her to bear. Her father once told her that willow trees grew in the spots that weeping mothers died. When she asked what they were weeping for, he said, "Their children." She pushed the thought out of her head. It was too much. "I want to go the way we came."

"But that way's farther."

"You go wherever you want. I'm going the way we came," Zee said. She'd had enough. She couldn't shake the image of that bloody-eyed dog and it hurt that Elijah didn't believe her. *This is what happens when you're always telling stories, Zee.* Was her imagination just in overdrive, like her sister always told her it was?

She shook her head. No. She knew what she saw. It was real.

"Zee?" Elijah said. "You okay?"

"I'm fine. I just . . ." She looked up at the willow tree again. "I don't want to go that way."

"Because of the dog?"

"Yeah," Zee lied. A breeze sent the willow tree's branches toward her, stretching like hundreds of arms. Without thinking, she stepped back to avoid their touch.

"Okay," Elijah said. "We'll take the long way." He said it like it was no big deal, and for that Zee was thankful.

On the walk home, Elijah told Zee the plot of the book he was reading—about some English girl who had a pet that could change shape. Something about fighting armored bears. There were no ghosts or monsters, so normally it wouldn't have been the kind of thing Zee would have cared about. But today, after what happened, it was nice to be quiet for a change.

And even when she caught sight of another shadow out of the corner of her eye, she bit her tongue and tried to just listen.

3

MOST EVERYTHING WAS CLEANED UP FROM THE STORM BY THE NEXT day, so that meant school was in session. Zee went through her morning trying not to think about the dog. While she knew what she'd seen in the cemetery, the farther she got from that moment the less real it seemed. It felt instead like something she'd watched on a movie screen. As the hours passed and day turned to night and night turned to day, she was mostly convinced that it had just been a trick of light. A shadow. It was probably just some poor old mangy thing that got loose in the storm and was lost. Poor thing was probably hungry. Or sick.

"Zera?"

In fact, she reasoned, by now someone would have probably put up a Lost Dog sign for the poor thing. With a reward. A hundred dollars for the safe return of . . . Pickles. Or Lucky. Or some other cute name like that.

"Zera!"

Zee jerked in her desk and snapped to attention in the classroom. "Yes?"

"It's time to go," Mr. Houston, her history teacher, said. The rest of the class was lined up near the door, jackets on, backpacks slouched on shoulders. Today was the trip upstate to the big library. How could she forget?

Knobb's Ferry didn't have much, but it had a library. Sadly, it was about the size of Zee's living room and only had two computers. The ladies who volunteered there were nice enough, but Zee had gone through every book in the children's section by the time she was in third grade. About an hour upstate in New Castle there was a real library. With three *floors*. It was the library that Zee always wanted to go to but rarely did. With Abby working as much as she did, it was hard to find the time to get all the chores and grocery shopping and homework done let alone an extra trip to the library. It was one of her favorite places on earth. And today, they were getting a backstage tour.

"I'm coming," Zee said, scrambling to get up and get her coat out of the cupboard.

"A touch distracted?" Mr. Houston said.

Zee scowled, grabbed her things, and lined up at the door behind Nellie Bloom. Nellie was perfect, or at least she acted like she was. Her strawberry-blond hair in perfect curls, her dress perfectly matched to her shoes. Zee shuffled behind her in her jeans, sneakers, and a T-shirt she already wore two . . . or maybe three . . . days in a row now. Nellie gave a condescending sniff because perfect Nellie, to be perfectly honest, hated Zee.

"Nice job, zoned out again, huh, *Zero*," she said with a muffled laugh, making the shape of an O with her hand.

"Shut up, Nellie."

And Zee, for the most part, hated her right back. It was a feud that had started a year earlier over something trivial. Since then it had blown up into an all-out war.

Mr. Houston led the classroom out to the waiting bus. The driver opened the door, and Mr. Houston said, "Where's Principal McCaffery? I thought he was coming with us."

"Beats me," the driver said.

Mr. Houston gave a quick worried glance around

the parking lot before muttering, "Strange," under his breath. He turned back to his class. "Let's go, kids."

They loaded onto the bus, and Zee didn't bother to search the rows for a familiar face. Elijah wasn't taking this trip with them. He was in advanced classes, and they had their own, better field trips. Like to the city for museums and science centers. That's what you got to do when you were *really* smart. Zee slipped into an open seat, scooting all the way in toward the window. Martin Pearsly sat down next to her, giving her a quick glance before burying his head in a book with a spaceship on the cover. Zee respected people that wanted to be left alone. She watched the landscape zip by, town turning into highway running past fields of grass. She let her mind wander back to a story she'd been thinking about and was deep into what Abby called "Planet Zee" by the time the bus pulled off the highway and dipped down the hill toward New Castle's public library. It was right on the river, so as they pulled into the parking lot, light bounced off the water and lit the building up. She tried to remember the last time she'd been here. It had to be before her father left to find work upstate. For a brief moment, Zee couldn't remember how long that had been. It felt like forever even though she knew it wasn't.

The bus door hissed open, and the sixth-grade class clambered off.

"Okay, line up," Mr. Houston was shouting as the class ignored him and gathered in groups. He finally got control of the situation and led them up the front steps toward the doors, where a woman in a red skirt and black blazer, hair in a braided halo, waited.

"Welcome to New Castle library," she said, holding her arms wide. "I'm Mrs. Washington, one of the archivists. Today we are going to have a tour of the parts of the building that the public doesn't usually get to see. But before we venture inside, I want you to take a look at the outside of the building. Notice anything interesting?"

Zee stared up at the wide, flat face of the building, two vast architectural wings jutting out on either side reaching back toward the water. There were quotes about reading carved into the walls and a large revolving door. Everyone near her shrugged and shuffled their feet.

"No one? For instance, the two wings on either side. Does that remind you of anything?"

Zee sighed and raised her hand. "An open book."

Mrs. Washington lit up. "Yes, that's correct. Did everyone hear? The library was designed to mimic an open book with these two wings acting as the covers

26

and the front being similar to a spine. I'm delighted you noticed."

Nellie Bloom muttered something under her breath, but Zee didn't catch it as they followed Mrs. Washington into the building. The truth was, her father had told her that little nugget of trivia years ago. He had a thing for useless trivia, especially about art and architecture. She missed him so badly sometimes—like right this second—that the ache knotted in her chest like a second heart. Her sadness was a thing she couldn't figure out how to carry.

The lobby was grand and ornate, two marble staircases leading off to the left and right. Down the hall you could hear the noise from the children's room, but here in the lobby all was deliciously quiet. Ahead of her Zee could see a wide reading room with majestic columns and big red reading chairs. In the center was a round wooden pen inside which people were working, checking out and returning the public's books. Mrs. Washington ushered them into a side office where they left their coats and their lunches. Before they started, she gave everyone a small slip of paper that contained a series of letters and numbers: a call number.

"We're going to be using those later, so be sure to put it somewhere safe," she said.

27

The tour took them through the public areas first, the art department and the history department, before dovetailing through literature. It was there at the back of the literature department that they passed through a door marked "Library Employees Only."

Zee had never been in any of the behind-the-scenes spaces of the library, and she was giddy down to her bones. Mrs. Washington herded the class onto a freight elevator. It was the old kind that had a large metal grate that groaned and came slamming down like a guillotine after the door closed, startling the class. Mrs. Washington smiled. "Just a noisy old thing. Nothing to worry about."

The gears roared to life, sounding like a monster waking up as they plunged downward.

"These are called the decks. They are mainly storage areas. We have four stories' worth of decks under the library, which means more of this library is underground than aboveground."

Zee let those words sink in as the elevator came to a stop and groaned open. The decks were darker than upstairs, and exit arrows were marked across the floor. The shelves were metallic and bursting with books, most of which were coated in a fine layer of dust. It was more than a little spooky.

"These are items that we need to keep but that

don't get as much use as the more popular items upstairs. If patrons are interested in seeing them, we send down a page to bring the book up to them. We also keep rare books in a special room down here. Follow me."

They wove through the stacks, the ceiling low. There were small metal staircases here and there leading deeper underground.

"It's gross down here," someone muttered. Steve Cotter pulled a book from a shelf and blew the dust off it, which caused Amanda Peal to erupt into a sneezing fit. Before Mrs. Washington could see, Mr. Houston snatched the book away from him and returned it to the shelf with a stern look. Mrs. Washington chattered on at the front talking about the foundation of the building and how long it had been around for. She mentioned that with the river right next to them, extra protection had to be built to ensure that the decks would not flood.

With a shiver, Zee pictured all those beautiful books floating underwater, their pages fanning out like the hair of a mermaid.

"Come now, follow me," Mrs. Washington chirped as her heels clicked down the metal staircase to the next deck. It was even darker and dustier down here. The class followed her down the steps. At the end of each row was a small timer dial. As she turned dials, the light in each row flicked on. "We have timers down here to ensure that we are not wasting electricity."

The timers ticked a slow, steady pulse that Zee found unnerving. Because Mrs. Washington couldn't turn them all on at the same time, instead of just ticking to one beat it sounded like rapid fire. Tick-atickatickaticka. *How strange*, Zee thought, *to feel so out of place in a space I love so much.* It was a cold feeling, like an ice cube in her belly, something she didn't recall feeling before. That is, prior to yesterday in the cemetery . . .

"Now," Mrs. Washington said, "before we go to the Morgue—"

"MORGUE!" Amanda Peal shouted as the rest of the class descended into chatter.

Nellie crossed her arms and said, "So immature."

"Quiet, quiet," Mr. Houston said, shushing the group.

"Yes, yes," Mrs. Washington said with her hands up. "I know it's a strange term. The Morgue is our archival storage area. It's a newspaper term for the storage space in which old papers are kept, so we've adopted that term for this space. So," she said, "no dead bodies or anything. Though I will say, since it's October, rumor has it this whole building is haunted."

"Haunted?" said Clare Wrobleski. "What do you mean 'haunted'?"

"Oh, just stories about workers who died during the construction of this building or older librarians who keeled over and didn't realize they were dead." Mrs. Washington chuckled, but the kids looked serious. "It's an old building. Old buildings carry a lot of history. But I assure you there is nothing in this place that will hurt you." Mrs. Washington clasped her hands together. "Now before we go on, take out those slips of paper that I gave you at the beginning of the tour."

Zee pulled her slip out of her pocket. 398.25 R was written in neat handwriting.

"We're going on a little scavenger hunt. So let's see if you can find the item attached to that call number." Mrs. Washington produced a small box of little pencils, which the class took and passed around. "The items I selected for you are fragile, but not too fragile. Once you locate them, write down the title and author from the spine. DON'T remove anything from its resting place . . . er, shelves. We'll meet back here in ten minutes."

The class dispersed, some excited, others lagging behind and complaining about being bored. Zee glanced down at her call number, and then searched the shelves for direction. Her call number pulled her farther from the group, out to where the timer lights had not been turned on yet. She turned the dial just like Mrs. Washington had, and a splash of light and the ticking of the timer filled the aisle.

This must be what it's like to be a librarian, she thought. It seemed like a good job if you had to have a job. Unless of course, you could make storytelling your job. Getting paid to tell stories seemed to Zee like a dream come true.

She continued down the long row of shelves, moving between the dusty tomes, getting farther from the group. The rest of the rows were still dark, and for a second she was sure she saw snatches of shadow moving between the stacks. Her arms were awash with goose bumps, and her breath hitched in her throat. It was hard not to think of the cemetery shadows and the hound. She turned the dial on the edge of the next row, but nothing happened. Zee glanced down the long dark row of books and then steeled herself and kept walking.

It's just a library, she thought. *You're being silly.* But it was still there, that cold rush in the belly feeling. One step after another and she reached the end of the dark row. She glanced back and swore she saw another shadow move, slipping like a ghost between the shelves. It made the hairs on her arms stand up.

But at the next row, the dial worked, and she was warmed by the wash of light. The shadows retreated in the new light, and things that looked creepy morphed back into books and shelves. Now the ticking timer sounded comforting, a gentle tapping in the background. She checked the spines of the books nearest to her.

377, 378, 378.5, 378.56 . . .

Finally, she reached the 398s. Her finger tracked the call numbers until she located the slender hardback book that matched hers. She glanced up and down the aisle but saw no one. She wasn't supposed to touch the book, she knew that, and yet, up went her hand plucking it off the shelf. The binding was loose, the first pages cracked from age. There was a brown mottling, like spiderwebs, on the pages. She paused, feeling watched. That cold feeling morphed into something else. Something close by.

"That's called foxing," a voice behind her said. "And you're not supposed to be touching that book."

Zee nearly leaped out of her skin. She spun around, almost dropping the book. There was a boy standing there. He wore a white shirt tucked into dusty brown pants and, strangely, suspenders. *Who wears suspenders?*

"Man, you scared me," Zee said, still clutching the book tightly.

"I'm awfully sorry about that. But you're not supposed to be touching these books. They're fragile."

Did he have an accent? The light timers continued to tick through the silence.

"I'm Paul," he said, leaning against the book stacks. "I work here."

"You seem really young to have a job."

Paul smiled in turn. "I'm older than I look." He eyed the book in her hands again.

"I'm on a class trip," Zee said, glancing down the aisle. The timers behind her clicked off, plunging everything around her aisle into darkness. "We had to go and find a book."

"Which one did you find?" Paul asked, his smile making his dimples show. He seemed nice, unlike most of the kids in her school. Like someone that she and Elijah would want to hang out with. Zee realized that was a feeling she had so rarely. She couldn't help but smile.

"It's called . . ." Zee turned the page carefully.

"Careful, she's very old," Paul said.

"*Spirits and Illusions: Science During the Age of*

Metaphysics by Charles Roebling."

"What's the date on that?" Paul asked.

"1866."

"She *is* old."

"Yeah," Zee said with a smile. "She is." Zee liked that Paul referred to the book as "she." It was sort of cool. "What do you do here, Paul?"

"Me? Oh, this and that. I manage the lights and the water system. Make sure the boiler doesn't kick out in the winter. Keep the old girl running."

"How did you know that was called foxing?"

"You been round long as I have, you pick up a thing or two about books."

And then the light in Zee's aisle cut off, plunging them into darkness. A small, startled cry escaped her lips. When the lights came back on just as quickly, her head whipped around toward the end of the aisle and a figure standing there, silhouetted by the darkness.

"Who are you talking to?" Nellie said, her hand still on the dial.

Zee glanced back, but Paul was gone. Utterly vanished. She peeked between the rows of books—still nothing.

"He was . . ." Zee said, confused before composing herself and adding, "No one."

"Were you talking to *yourself*?" Nellie said with a

laugh. "Oh my goodness, Zero, that is a new low, even for you."

Zee slipped the book back on the shelf and stomped down the aisle, nudging past Nellie, who was blocking her path.

"You weren't supposed to touch the books, Zero. My aunt works here, and she can totally get you thrown out."

Wow, she disliked this girl. "Then go tell on me."

Zee, followed by Nellie, caught up with the rest of the class in the Morgue.

"I found her, Mr. Houston," Nellie announced to the room, with a smug teacher's-pet look on her face.

"I need you to stay with the class, Zera," Mr. Houston chided.

While the name "Morgue" conjured up some intense images, the reality was pretty dull. Just shelves with boxes on them and long, flat filing cabinets filled with photos. Mrs. Washington was showing the class how an archivist processes a collection.

"Now, not only has the binding come loose but the first few pages as well as the front cover are detached. This is a very old book, and at this point we would have to place it in an archival box for protection. We would also limit the public's access to this material because it is so fragile."

"What's the point, then?" David Cotter asked. "Why keep it if no one can read it?"

"Because libraries not only serve as hubs of the community but also as institutions that bear witness to history."

"And you know what happens if you forget history," Mr. Houston said. The class groaned and answered, "You're doomed to repeat it."

Mrs. Washington chuckled. "Indeed. You don't see the signs, the ways in which you make the same mistakes, the ways the path before you is lined by those that came before. It's a powerful lesson, children. Now then, where were we? Oh yes," she said. "You see these brown marks?" Mrs. Washington held up the book to the class. "These are called—"

"Foxing," Zee blurted out, and then quickly turned red.

Mrs. Washington gave her a measured look. "Yes, that's right. I've never met anyone outside the business that knew that term. Do you have archivists in your family?"

"No," Zee said, regretting that she spoke.

"She doesn't even have a family," Nellie muttered from the back. Zee turned around and shot her a look.

"Well then. I do believe it is time for lunch!" Mrs.

Washington said, ushering them out of the Morgue and back up the winding staircases into the light of the main library. As she passed through the stacks, Zee searched for Paul. But she saw nothing but shadows.

An hour later, as they were getting back on the bus, Nellie sidled up to Zee once again.

"What do you want?" Zee said.

"Who were you really talking to downstairs?"

"I said no one."

"No, you said 'he was.' So who were you talking to?"

"Can't we just go back to mutually hating each other? 'Cause that was fun," Zee said as she boarded the bus. But she knew it was too late. She'd been through this before. Once Nellie latched on to something, she was like a dog with a bone. She wouldn't let go.

"Okay, everyone, get your seats," Mr. Houston was yelling as the sixth-grade class clambered and fought for seats. Zee slipped into the first one she saw and scooted down low. Nellie got in the seat behind her with Liza Cleary. Ten minutes into the ride, they were having a purposefully loud conversation. Loud enough to make sure Zee heard it.

"And she was talking to *no one*," Nellie said.

"Well," Liza chimed in, "she is 'Zero' 'cause she has absolutely zero friends."

"She can't even be her own friend!" Nellie said loudly. "You know, calling her Zero is fun, but I think I've got a better name."

Zee sunk farther down in her seat. She hated the girl.

"What's that?" Liza asked.

Fuming, Zee sat up in her seat and spun around. "Yeah, Nellie, what's that?"

Nellie cocked an eyebrow, and the two girls stared at each other for several beats before Nellie smiled and said, "Ghost Girl."

Liza exploded in a peal of laughter. "That's perfect!"

Unable to come up with a retort, Zee rolled her eyes and slumped down in her chair. The chatter started immediately. Someone at the back of the bus asked what Nellie and Liza were laughing at, and before she knew it, the whole bus was asking who Ghost Girl was. She tried to put on an air of disinterest, but inside it burned. It burned through her belly and up her throat. Then the burning moved to the back of her eyes, where it threatened to spill out.

By the time they got back to school, the whole bus

was in on the "Ghost Girl" thing. Zee beelined it back into the building as soon as Mr. Houston finished the head count. She went straight to her locker to pick up her books for last period, determined to somehow get through this day.

"Ghost Girl?" Elijah said as he slid up next to Zee at her locker after last bell.

"Stop," Zee said. "I'm not in the mood."

"What happened?" he asked, adjusting the bag on his shoulder.

"Nothing happened, okay?"

"Zee," he said as they headed down the hall toward the main lobby. "It's *me* you're talking to."

Someone passed and bumped Zee's shoulder and then let out a bone-chilling "ooooohhhh!" and the rest of the lobby started laughing.

Zee and Elijah didn't talk much on the bus ride home, but when they got off and it was finally just the two of them heading down Hickory Lane, Zee opened up.

"There was this guy, in the stacks. He said his name was Paul. He said that he worked for the library."

"Okay, so he probably did."

"Right, but when Nellie showed up and flipped on the timer lights, he was gone," Zee said. "Just completely gone. He was standing right next to me and

40

the light went out and when it came back on a second later he was *gone*."

"He probably just left. Maybe he had work to do," Elijah offered.

"Maybe," Zee said, hoping she could arrange her face to make it look like she agreed. It wasn't that. Paul didn't seem old enough to even work there. And the way he was dressed. The way he talked. Zee shook her head and put it out of her mind. She was letting Nellie Bloom get to her.

"Anyway," Elijah continued, "even if . . ." He didn't finish the sentence, as if somehow saying it would make it seem too real. "You know what's the great thing about being Ghost Girl?"

Zee scowled. "Um, nothing."

"Nah. Now you get to haunt them." He held up his fist, and Zee smiled as she bumped it.

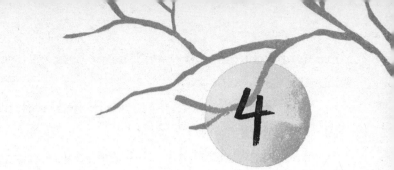

ELIJAH AND ZEE DROPPED THEIR SCHOOLBAGS BY HIS FRONT DOOR and beelined for the fridge.

"This whole Ghost Girl thing is going to blow over," Elijah said. "Don't even worry about it. I know how to handle these people."

But Zee was worried. Nellie was determined to make her sixth-grade life as miserable as possible.

"I mean, I don't care," Zee said, trying to sound casual. Elijah gave her a look, and she frowned. Was it that obvious? That was the thing about Elijah. He had his fair share of bullies, but he always seemed to be able to stay one step ahead of them. For Zee it felt like she was drowning in a sea of Nellie hate.

"Off topic, did I tell you about Mrs. Mamson, the shop teacher?"

"The egg drop?"

"Yeah. This is not going to work. I'm going to fail."

"Elijah, you've never failed anything," Zee said, but she knew Elijah was worried. Everyone in sixth grade had to go through the egg drop. Elijah's turn was in less than two weeks, when Mrs. Mamson was going to climb out on the roof of the school and drop an egg—literally—off the side of the building. It was the job of the student to build some kind of container so that the egg would land safely and not crack open when it hit the sidewalk.

"My first attempt involved a parachute, but in test runs it failed to open. Now I have a capsule that's padded. I just don't get it. How is this the kind of thing the administration deems useful?" Elijah asked as they headed into the kitchen. "I hate shop. Building things is not my strong suit. I like solving puzzles and sorting things out. Real problems that affect real people."

Elijah yanked open the fridge, and he and Zee stared into the near empty shelves. "Problems like 'Why are there never any snacks in this fridge?'" Zee said.

"Exactly," Elijah laughed.

"Hey, how was school?" Elijah's father asked from the doorway. Mr. Turner was a big guy, muscular and tall, and he filled the doorway in a way that made Zee feel trapped. She wondered if that was the way Elijah felt all the time.

Zee watched Elijah exhale slowly. "Fine, Dad."

"Hi, Mr. Turner," Zee said. Elijah's father gave her a once-over, a tight smile, and then turned back to his son.

"You going to pick something or just waste all my electricity?" he asked, taking a seat at the table and opening the newspaper. Thankfully, Mr. Turner was too far away to hear the things Elijah muttered under his breath. "Let's go. Pick something or close it."

Zee remembered when Elijah told her how much a room changed when his father was in it. The kitchen was a place where Elijah and his mother used to bake and cook and listen to music and laugh. But now that his father spent more time in the kitchen, it was the opposite of all that. It was a joyless place. No air. No laughter.

Zee could see why.

Elijah often said his dad still liked to talk about one specific game against Derby High that they would have won if the coach hadn't pulled him out in the last quarter. Now that he couldn't play football, Martin Turner loved nothing more than cars. He worked at the mechanic shop in town. As a kid he used to drag race them. He and his friends would work on the engines, souping them up, and then they would race, hitting the brakes hard at the end, leaving a trail of burnt rubber. Elijah told Zee all his dad's stories. He only appreciated things you could do with your body, and your hands. It was the same thing with the egg drop and shop class. It was everything Elijah was not. And that was the problem.

"Come on, let's go to my room."

As they passed him, Mr. Turner said, "I was thinking of hitting the gym this evening. You interested?"

"No," Elijah said.

"You didn't even need to think about it, eh?"

"Nope," Elijah said, moving toward the door.

"Look, Elijah. I was once . . . like you." Elijah froze in place. Zee could see in his eyes that he was begging his father to stop. She wished she could make them both disappear. "I'm just saying it doesn't have to be like this. We can get you jogging. Or spend a couple hours on the weight machines. Zee can come with us! Wouldn't that be fun?"

Neither Zee nor Elijah responded.

"It'll feel good. Doing something with your hands. Breaking a sweat. It changed my life. . . ." Here he just trailed off.

Elijah broke the awkward silence. "Dad, we have a project to work on, so can we talk about this later?"

"I'm just saying that I understand, okay? I do. I'm trying to help you."

"Where's Mom?" Elijah asked, changing the subject.

"Your mother is lying down," his father said, breaking eye contact and turning the pages of the paper without reading. "Best not to bother her."

Zee knew that Elijah's mother had been *lying down* for a few weeks now. At one point, Elijah even said he was afraid that she was dying. It scared Zee too, thinking about him losing his mother, especially because they had always been so close. And she understood why. Mrs. Turner had been *fun*. She made up holidays and decorated the house for no reason. She let him stay up late to finish the books he was reading. She would even pick a random day during the school year when Elijah didn't have to go to school. It was their special day to do whatever he wanted. In Zee's eyes, Mrs. Turner was the best mom in the world. She was jealous of what they had.

What she could never have with her own mom.

Elijah headed down the hall as his father called after him, "Don't bother her."

"Bother?" Elijah repeated softly, just so Zee could hear. "How am I a bother?" At his parents' door, Elijah turned to Zee and whispered, "I need you to keep watch."

"What?"

"Just keep an eye out for my father. Let me know if he comes down the hall."

"Maybe I should just go wait in your room."

"I never ask you to do anything for me," Elijah said. "I'm asking now. Please. Just let me know if he's coming."

"Okay." Zee nodded.

Elijah opened the door, and Zee could see that the small light on the nightstand was on. A dehumidifier hummed in the corner of the room. All Zee could see was a lump in the bed. A snatch of loose brown curls.

"Mom?" Elijah whispered. "You up?"

Even from the doorway the air smelled stale. Waxy. Zee could see a pile of balled-up tissues on the nightstand.

"Mom?"

The lump in the bed stirred. Zee watched Elijah kneel down.

She must have opened her eyes because he smiled and said, "Hey, Mom. You doing okay?"

But she didn't answer. Or at least, not from what Zee could tell.

"Mom?" he said, shaking her shoulder gently. "You awake?" Zee read once that sometimes people opened their eyes while they were sleeping. It was a creepy concept. It made her think that they would look dead, like someone who should be in a coffin. But even from the doorway Zee could see that Elijah's mother didn't look dead.

She looked hollow.

Like her body was still there but the thing that made her his mom had floated too far away to find its way back to her eyes.

Like a light had been switched off.

"Mom?" he said a little louder.

But she didn't respond. Elijah rubbed his eyes.

"Hey," his father hissed from right behind her, causing Zee to nearly jump out of her skin. "What did I say?"

Elijah stood up and crept out of the room. His father closed the bedroom door behind him. "What did I tell you?"

"What's wrong with her?"

"She's tired. She just needs some rest."

Is she dying? was the question Zee wanted to ask, but instead she said, "Is she going to be okay?"

"Yes. Of course. The doctor came round while you were at school. Gave her some new pills. He said they would help." His father clamped a wide hand on Elijah's shoulder, giving it a reassuring shake. "You know your mother. She's always doing too much. She needs to slow down. That's what the doctor says the pills are helping her do. She'll be fine soon."

When? Zee wondered. She looked at her friend, to see if he believed what his father was telling him, but all Zee saw was worry.

More than worry. Fear.

"I can order us a pizza," his father said.

"I'm not hungry," Elijah said, looking at the bedroom door.

"Ha," his father snorted. "Now I know that's not true. Elijah, you're *always* hungry," he said before heading down the hall. "I'll call you kids when it's here."

Elijah turned and went into his bedroom.

Zee followed him. "You okay?" she asked gently.

"I'm fine," Elijah said, but Zee knew he wasn't. He wouldn't even look at her. After a few beats, he said, "You know, actually, I have a lot of homework to do tonight, so I should probably get started."

"Oh, sure. Okay. I'll see you tomorrow, then?"

"Yeah, tomorrow."

Zee hesitated for a second before giving Elijah a quick hug, a gesture she hoped said everything she didn't have the words for right now. One that told him she was scared too. That they could be scared together. One that told him that someday things would get better.

"Hey," Zee said when they met up on the walk to the bus stop the next day. "You okay?" She nudged him with her elbow.

"Yeah," he said. "I'm fine. Just tired."

They walked in awkward silence as Zee debated a thousand different ways to bring up what had happened yesterday. Elijah didn't seem like he wanted to talk about it, but what if she was wrong? That was the thing about Elijah—he always knew how to get Zee to open up even when she didn't know she needed to talk. He was good like that. But she was the opposite. All awkward and blurting out the wrong thing at the wrong time.

"Hey, did you see that dog again?" Elijah asked, and Zee was thankful. This was a much easier topic, even if it terrified her.

"From the cemetery? No, why?"

"Last night, I thought I heard something," Elijah said. "Like a howling. I opened my window and stuck my head out, but the street was empty. When I closed it again and got back into bed, I heard it again just as I drifted off. It was weird."

"Yeah, that does seem weird. I, um, didn't hear anything," Zee said, which was a lie. She'd heard it too. It was low and jarring, and during the night, she could feel it in her bones. It sounded like it was right outside her bedroom window, but she wasn't brave enough to check. Instead she just squeezed her eyes shut and told herself that everything was okay.

By recess, Zee managed to put all of it out of her mind. The dog, Ghost Girl, Elijah's mother, the way Paul had just vanished into thin air. All of it. In fact, she was in the middle of a great story, having gathered a nice little group before her. It was a take on the classic "Monkey's Paw" story, which she'd discovered in a collection of scary stories. The gist is that a magic monkey's paw finds its way to a family who uses it to make wishes. They wish most of all for their son to come home, although he had died in a war. And then there's a knock at the door. Zee remembered getting to the end of the story, with the terrifying knock upon the front door, and shuddering. It was one story that never left her. And since then, she'd used it as inspiration. That was one of the things she loved about stories—they grew into more stories like wildflowers.

"No matter where he looked," Zee said, her small audience enraptured, "all he could see were the red eyes of the monkey's face. Down at the gym floor—monkey face. Up by the basketball nets? Monkey face! In fact, when he looked down at the assembly before him, the angry demon eyes of that cursed monkey stared right into his."

"Hey, Ghost Girl, you telling lies again?"

Zee stopped her story and looked up to see Nellie Bloom standing there with her arms crossed.

"Go away, Nellie," Zee said, angry that she broke the tension right when Zee had everyone transfixed.

"You shouldn't be talking like that."

Zee rolled her eyes and continued her story, but the audience was less attentive. Nellie had shattered the illusion and spoiled everything. She exchanged a frustrated look with Elijah.

"My mother," Nellie said loudly, "says there's no difference between a story and a lie. All of it is untrue."

Zee stopped and looked at the girl. She had brand-new shoes, clothes with designer labels. Her hair was fixed by a mother that probably doted over her. Zee felt her own hair slipping loose from the messy ponytail she'd managed before the bus came. Her sister was still asleep this morning after pulling a double shift at the diner. Zee's lunch was a possibly expired yogurt, a banana, and half a bagel—a mismatched collection of whatever she could find in the fridge. Zee hated Nellie Bloom. And it wasn't just because she had everything and Zee had nothing; it was because Nellie had everything and she was still dull as dull can be.

"Sounds like your mom never heard a good story, then. Too bad for her, I guess."

"Just admit it, Zero. You're a liar," Nellie said, her hands on her hips.

"No, I'm not," Zee said her face getting hot. "Lies hurt people. Stories help them. It's not my fault if you and your mom are too stupid to figure that out."

"Okay. Then what about that time you told everyone that there were cops here to arrest the librarian for being in charge of a cult?"

Everyone turned and looked at Zee.

"Or," Nellie continued, "what about the time when you said you had a fever so bad you dreamed that the butcher, Mr. Phelps, was going to die of a heart attack at his job and then it happened and you said you could predict people's futures."

"I . . ." Zee said, her face getting warm.

The kids around her laughed nervously, and it took a second before Zee realized they were laughing *at* her.

"Or what about yesterday at the library when you were talking to yourself?"

Someone in the crowd turned and said, "Wait, I thought you said she was talking to a ghost?" The rest of the kids snickered. "Right, Ghost Girl?"

"You're a liar, Zero," Nellie said, building on the momentum of the crowd—on what should have been *her* momentum. Then with a little laugh she said, "All those lies must have been what turned your hair so white."

When the rest of the kids laughed along with her, Zee grit her teeth.

"Go away, Nellie," Elijah said, but the girl ignored him. She was far too focused on Zee, a cruel glint in her eye. She was high off the attention.

Zee knew exactly what that felt like.

And Zee also knew that meant that this was not going to end well.

"I guess telling lies is what you have to do when you have nothing else in your life. No friends. No mother. And now . . . no father either. Where did he run off to again?"

"He's upstate looking for work. Not that it's any of your business."

"Work. Sure. That's not what my father said."

"I don't care what your father said, Nellie," Zee said, her hands curling into fists.

"He said that your father is upstate because he found himself a new wife. And he's got a whole other family with her."

There was a collective gasp from the kids that now formed a circle around the girls. Then smatterings of laughter. Zee could feel them looking at her, waiting for her to do something. Anything.

"You shut up, Nellie. You're the one lying."

"Oh yeah? 'Cause my dad does business in the city and he *saw* your dad there with a whole other family. He saw him with his own two eyes."

"My dad isn't in the city."

"Shame, really. Honestly, I feel bad for your sister. She didn't even graduate high school. Isn't that right?"

"You shut up about Abby," Zee said.

"Or what?"

"Or I'm going to shut you up."

"My mother said your sister will probably be pregnant in a year. She said your whole family is t-r-a-s-h. Starting with your moth—"

Zee launched herself at Nellie, her fists flying. Words were coming out of her mouth, but she was like a possessed thing—all she felt was the power of shoving Nellie down, of her fist connecting with the girl's body. At one point she had a whole hank of hair in her grip, and she pulled as hard as she could, reveling in the sound of Nellie's screams. When rough adult hands pulled her off the girl, she managed to get a final kick in, hitting Nellie squarely in the face. Blood gushed from the girl's nose.

Thirty minutes later, after being dragged down the hall by Ms. Levinson, the math teacher, Zee found herself sitting across from a very unamused Mr. Houston. Nellie was outside the door, a bloodied rag held to her face.

"Zera . . ."

It's Zee, she thought but didn't say. He wouldn't have listened anyway. Also Zee wasn't sure what her history teacher was doing sitting at the principal's desk.

"Where's Principal McCaffery?"

"That's not your concern. I'm in charge for the time being, and this is deeply troubling. A physical altercation with another student? Fighting, Zera? Do you think this is how good girls behave?"

Zee gave him a look but said nothing.

"Young ladies know how to keep their hands to themselves."

"Guess I'm not a girl, then," Zee muttered. If she weren't a girl, then she could beat Nellie Bloom to a pulp every day and everyone would excuse it as just something that boys do. Why was that? Why did boys get to behave badly but girls always had to be quiet and small and polite? Zee was none of those things. She never wanted to be them.

Later, sitting outside the principal's office, she silently recounted everything Nellie had said so that she could plan her revenge. She was going to get that girl. It had gone on too long. It started with the teasing in gym about the hair on Zee's legs. It was like, in that moment, Nellie *saw* Zee and since then she couldn't unsee her. Like she was laser-focused on her. Then she started with that Zero nickname, which caught on with the whole grade, and now she was calling her Ghost Girl. But more than anything, Zee couldn't stand the way she talked about her family. Zee knew other people in town talked. She was used to the pitying looks, even though she hated them. She knew Abby got them too, but Abby always seemed to be able to ignore it.

What other people say about me is none of my business, her sister always said. *And it's none of your business either.*

But it *felt* like her business. And now stories about Dad leaving them. That one burrowed deep inside her. In fact, it reminded her how long it had been since he'd even called. Abby had told her last week that he got some work on a long-haul trucking company and that meant he was driving most days and nights, but still. How hard was it to check in? Didn't he want to know if she was okay? If Abby was okay?

A whole other family.

The words burned inside her. Yes, she was going to get Nellie Bloom back and that would be the thing everyone would be talking about. She'd need Elijah's help of course, but she was going to plan the best prank this town had ever seen. The whole school would be talking about it *years* from now.

"Let's go." Abby stood over Zee, a very unhappy look on her face. She had just come out of the office with Mr. Houston. "Now."

"Abby." Mr. Houston stood in the doorway of the principal's office looking at Zee. "I do hope you'll implement some of the practices we talked about."

"Of course. And again, thank you."

What was she thanking him for? Zee wondered with a scowl, but she knew better than to utter a single word. She had to be invisible if she was going to avoid her sister's wrath. When they got in the car, her sister turned to her.

Here we go, Zee thought.

"I . . ." Abby rubbed her forehead and sighed loudly. "I don't even know what to do with you anymore."

"Abby . . ."

"No. Listen to me. You're fighting now? You have detention for the next week. I hope you realize that the *only* reason you weren't suspended was because I had to beg Mr. Houston."

"He's not even the principal."

"I don't really care. You made me miss work, *again*, and now I have to find a way to make up those hours. What is wrong with you?"

"It wasn't my fault."

Abby laughed. But not in a good way. She laughed in a fed-up, what's-happened-to-my-life?, my-sister-is-an-idiot sort of way. "It's *never* your fault. 'It wasn't my fault' will be written on your tombstone."

"No, really, Abby. Nellie Bloom started the whole thing."

"Did she? And I see you finished it by smashing her nose open."

"That was technically an accident."

"Oh. Well, it's technically not an accident that you're grounded for a week. No television. No after school time. No hanging out with Elijah."

"Abby, come on."

"No books!"

Zee shot her sister a look. "THAT'S NOT FAIR."

"Guess what?" Abby said, starting the car. "I don't really care."

They didn't talk the rest of the ride home, or at the house, or during all of dinner, which was comprised of microwaved leftover spaghetti that Abby brought home from the diner. Zee pushed the pasta around her plate wondering how it was possible for the sauce to be scalding in one part and freezing in another. Zee hated when she brought home food like this. The thought that she was eating someone else's leftovers grossed her out. Abby always told her it wasn't from stuff left on the plate, but from stuff that was fine but sent back to the kitchen, but Zee didn't believe her then and she certainly didn't believe her tonight. Eating someone else's food was gross. And below that, Zee burned with shame that this was something that Abby thought they needed to resort to. She thought about Nellie and her stupid new clothes, and her stomach burned from more than just the simultaneously undercooked and overcooked noodles.

"Finish your food," Abby said, breaking the silence.

"I'm not hungry."

"Fine," Abby said, snatching Zee's plate away and then dumping it into the garbage. "Happy?"

"Yes!" Zee spat back.

"Are you going to tell me what this fight was about?"

"Will that mean I'm not punished?"

"No."

"Then no."

"Zee," Abby said, sounding weary. She rubbed her eyes. "I want to know what Nellie said to you that made you so mad you punched her in the nose."

"First of all, I didn't punch her. I kicked her, and like I told you, it was by accident. Not that you ever listen to anything I say."

Abby sighed and looked out the window. "I am listening to you, Zee. I'm trying to understand what happened that you're getting into fights. This is not like you."

Maybe it is, Zee thought but didn't say. Maybe kicking Nellie in the face is exactly what she was like.

Goodness knows doing it felt great. It was the best way of shutting her up. "If I tell you what she said, will you believe me?"

"Yes."

"She called me a liar."

"Zee, that's no reason—"

"See! You're not even listening to my side."

"Okay, I'm sorry," Abby said, holding up her hands and then crossing her arms, "I'm listening."

Zee made sure Abby was serious before continuing. "She said that her father saw Dad in the city with a whole other family."

"What? That's . . . Zee, you know that's not true. Dad is upstate looking for work."

"Yeah, sure," Zee said. It came out sounding sarcastic.

"Hey, Zee, don't do that. Nellie Bloom's a liar. Her father's a liar. I'll go over there right now and tell him so myself. Dad is upstate looking for work. He loves us. He doesn't have a secret other family. That's nonsense!"

Zee stared out the window.

"But that still isn't a reason to fight with someone. You don't hit people, Zee. Use your words. Use that clever mind of yours to fight them."

"That wasn't all."

"What else?"

"She said you didn't graduate high school. . . ."

A pained look flashed across Abby's face but disappeared just as quickly. "You know that's temporary. You know I'm working on getting my GED. I just haven't had a chance to study with the shifts at work. . . ." Abby trailed off.

"And . . ." Zee paused before continuing ". . . she said her mother said . . . that you'd probably be pregnant in a year. She called us . . . trash."

Abby got up from the table and turned her back to Zee. She stared out the kitchen window for a while before she said, "Why don't you go up to your room?"

"I knew you wouldn't believe me," Zee muttered as she headed toward the stairs.

"I believe you, Zee," her sister said, still facing away from her. Even though she couldn't see her, Zee could tell she was about to cry. She could hear the tightness in her voice, and she hated it. "And listen . . . you can read, okay? But no television."

Zee climbed the stairs to her bedroom, her stomach in knots. She hated what Nellie brought into this house. Sure, things weren't great, but they were managing. Now Nellie ruined that too. A revenge plan hatched in the back of Zee's head. It was a delicious, awful plan, and Nellie Bloom was going to be sorry she ever said anything about Zee or her family.

5

NOW THAT THE STORM HAD PASSED AND THE ROADS HAD BEEN cleaned for the most part, people started to take stock of what had been lost. There were avenues that needed work, downed trees that needed to be cut up, sections of town that had lost power, but the thing no one was expecting was the fact that both Miss Jameson and Principal McCaffery were *missing*.

Deanna Jameson was a perky kindergarten teacher. She'd moved to town just a few years earlier and rented an apartment over the barbershop. When she didn't report to school and it became clear she was missing, the police went to her apartment. There was no sign of a struggle or anything like that.

It was more like Deanna just vanished.

Like a ghost.

And the same with Principal McCaffery. He was an all right principal, kind of like a more boring version of a teacher—though Zee never understood the hat thing. Principal McCaffery was obsessed with making sure that no one was wearing a baseball hat. It was the weirdest thing. He called them disruptive. Said that wearing a hat in class meant you wouldn't learn anything. But Zee figured if you didn't learn anything, it was probably because the teacher was lousy. Or because you weren't paying attention. What's a hat got to do with it?

Now the two of them were gone. Poof. Disappeared in the middle of the night. So naturally the entire town was talking about it. In detention, Zee even heard the other teachers going on about it.

"I knew she was trouble," Mrs. Matthews, the Spanish teacher, said. "I knew from the minute she came to town. You always have to be wary of a girl on her own like that."

Zee paused her homework to roll her eyes. Grownups were the worst. They'll throw anyone under the bus, especially women. She imagined for a moment what it must be like to live in a place with so many people that you could go missing and no one noticed.

She couldn't decide if that was worse or better, but she was leaning toward better.

"But her supervisor?" Mrs. Matthews continued.

Her companion, the hall monitor Mr. Chess, nodded.

"The whole thing is downright shameful. I can only think something must have been going on for months. Probably since she ran the fundraiser for the school vegetable garden."

"Disrespectful," Mr. Chess said, clucking his tongue.

Zee sighed. The only thing that seemed disrespectful to her were two old gossips talking about other people's lives. This, Zee reasoned, was the problem with small towns. When nothing happens, a thing like people moving away or moving on becomes the talk of the town. It's like they were jealous because they were still stuck here. The idea of someone else getting out and making something of their lives really chapped their butts.

Zee giggled to herself. That was a good expression. She'd have to be sure to use it again.

"Zera!" Mrs. Matthews snapped. "Pay attention to what you're doing."

"Yes, ma'am," Zee muttered.

The following morning, Zee woke feeling like she'd hardly slept at all. Everything felt fuzzy, and while she wasn't positive, she thought she heard the howling again. It was lodged in her memory the way a stubborn pebble gets stuck in the grooves of your sneaker. She remembered sitting up in bed, feeling like the sound was inside her filling her whole head. She even remembered putting her hands over her ears as if that could stop it. Dragging a brush through her uncooperating hair, she decided it was just a bad dream. A very bad dream, but a dream all the same. It just felt easier that way. When Zee came downstairs for breakfast, her sister eyed her. "You've worn that shirt three times this week."

"So?"

"So go put on something clean."

"Abby . . ."

"I'm serious, Zee. You can't go to school in that dirty T-shirt again. Go find something decent. Also don't you have an assembly today? I got an email about the new principal starting."

"So?"

"So, I don't want you looking like a slob. It's bad enough you got detention. You need to make a better impression, Zee. Now, go."

Zee stomped up the stairs knowing that this was

just another thing that Nellie caused. She knew that Abby was upset that someone was talking about them. Judging them. Zee rooted around in her drawer until she found a clean T-shirt and pulled it on, mumbling that Nellie won again. She was going to get that girl for sure.

By 11:30, the whole school piled into the gym, filling up the bleachers. Everyone had to sit with their class, but Zee spied Elijah a couple rows below her and waved. She also spotted Nellie, whose nose was still bandaged up. *Good for her*, Zee thought. She couldn't wait to get this day over with so she could talk to Elijah. Her revenge plan was coming together. Nellie Bloom was going to be sorry she ever messed with Zee.

Mr. Houston was at the front of the auditorium, trying, and mostly failing, to silence the kids on the bleachers. "Now, now, children, listen up," Mr. Houston said into the microphone. It screeched with feedback, and the kids quieted down, covering their ears.

"That's better. As some of you may have heard, Principal McCaffery had a . . . well . . . a . . . family situation. . . ." Mr. Houston cleared his throat and kept talking like the whole school didn't know he skipped town. "And he's been called away. The Hudson County Department of Education has hired a new principal. So if you could please, put your hands together and give a warm Knobb's Ferry Elementary School welcome to Principal Scratch!"

The double wide doors to the gymnasium flew open with a bang, causing a collective gasp among the students. Through the doors came a man unlike anyone Zee had ever seen. He was tall and thin, ghostly pale, with slicked-back hair. He was clean-shaven with a youthful face, and he wore dark sunglasses. He was dressed in head-to-toe black: black shirt, black pants, black jacket. The only spot of color came from his right hand, on which he wore a red glove. He walked like a cowboy, like a gunslinger, his boot heels clicking across the gymnasium floor.

He didn't go to the podium or shake Mr. Houston's hand. He strode right past Zee's history teacher until he was standing directly in front of the gathered schoolchildren. There was a beat. And then another. He gazed out at the children, and she could see their rows reflected in his sunglasses. The tension was so thick Zee thought if someone didn't say something she was going to scream.

"Do you love me?" he asked, arms raised, and Zee

had to choke back a laugh. "I can't hear you! I said, do you love me?"

There were a few stifled laughs from the audience and much fidgeting and shuffling of feet. But Zee sat up taller, a wide grin plastered on her face. She knew another storyteller when she saw one, and she could tell: this silver-tongued principal was a master.

"Well, I love you. And I love this town and this school and these teachers." He pointed toward the row of stunned-looking teachers behind him. "But most of all I love you. Because you deserve to be loved. You deserve to love yourself and you deserve to love each other."

Principal Scratch paced the floor, his hands folded behind him, that one red glove seeming to glow. He took off his sunglasses and said, "That's the kind of environment I want in this school. The kind I was hoping for. But I'm afraid I have heard that there isn't much love in this school these days. That there are people who hurt one another, students who are mean. What is that old saying? Sticks and stones can break my bones, but words can never hurt me. Hmmmm." He stopped and faced the students again. "Words can never hurt me. You," he said, spinning around and pointing at Stanley Brewster. "What's your name?"

Twisting his hands nervously, Stanley squeaked out his name.

"Well, Stanley," Principal Scratch continued. "What do you think of that saying? Do you think words can never hurt you?"

"Um, um . . ." Stanley trailed off, looking around the room, clearly hoping someone would save him. "I guess not."

"Has anyone ever said anything that made you sad, Stanley? Or mad?"

"Well, sure."

"Has anyone said anything that made you so mad you wanted to hurt them as much as they hurt you? Maybe hurt them even more. Why should they get to be the mean ones, right? We can all be mean, can't we?"

Stanley was practically thrumming with nervousness, and Principal Scratch laughed a low cool laugh as he watched the boy dangle like a worm on a fishing line. Principal Scratch put his red glove on the boy's shoulder, squeezed, and then, with the slightest bit of pressure, eased the boy back down onto the bleacher. When he did that, Zee swore she saw something, some faint shimmer of light zip past him.

Principal Scratch clasped his hands together and

inhaled deeply, like he was smelling the sweetest of flowers. "Then words can hurt you. Words can hurt you. Words *do* hurt you. Words can make you want to hurt others. What you say matters, children. And some here, some among you, choose to use words to *hurt* one another." On the word "hurt" Principal Scratch pounded his fist into his gloved hand for emphasis.

Zee felt a flush in her belly. Was he talking about her? She looked over to where Nellie was sitting and found to her surprise that Nellie met her gaze. Was she wondering the same thing? Zee couldn't tell if she was feeling the same way or not before Nellie broke the stare and turned back to Principal Scratch.

"Teasing that leads to name-calling. Name-calling that leads to pushing. Pushing that leads to hitting. Hitting that leads to fighting. All of this raw violence. And it all starts with one mean word. That is how bullying works. And maybe you think your classmates will help, stop things from escalating. Maybe they will stop the bully? Tell the teacher? But you must remember that no one will look out for you the same way *you* can. Sometimes to just survive you have to think of yourself first. You have to protect yourself."

There was an uncomfortable shifting among the other teachers.

"Raise your hands, children! Raise them up!" Principal Scratch said, his own red-gloved hand shooting into the air. The kids looked around at each other before slowly raising a hand in the air. "We are going to make a vow, here and now, to use our words for good and not harm. To take responsibility for ourselves. To protect *ourselves*. We're not going to wait for our friends, our classmates, to stand up. You must stand for you! Stand for you!"

The whole auditorium was chanting the slogan, and Principal Scratch stood before them, his arms stretched out wide, like it was a big wave of goodness coming at him. Zee swore she could see that shimmer again, just a flicker of light passing across the gymnasium. When the chanting died down, Principal Scratch said, "Who among you is brave enough to tell your story? Who wants to come up here and tell me about an experience you had where you had to stand up for what you wanted? What you needed?"

There was a ruckus at the bottom of the bleachers and Zee watched in amazement as Elijah pushed his way forward and up to Principal Scratch.

"Now, my friend, tell me, who is your bully?" Principal Scratch clamped that gloved hand on Elijah's shoulder and Elijah looked at it and then at Principal Scratch and without hesitation he said, "My father!"

Zee's jaw nearly hit the floor. She couldn't believe he would say that in front of the whole school.

"Yes," Principal Scratch said, slipping his sunglasses back on. "Good. Very good." A murmur rose from the crowd, building until it was a wave of voices, all different kids answering the question that Principal Scratch asked. "Yes. Indeed, my child, we must talk. Tell me what you need, what you want the most, and I will tell you how you can get it. Demand it. Take it." He turned back to the room and said, "I'm going to need to speak to all your parents. But you must remember, you can tell me anything. In fact, I hope each of you will tell me *everything*."

LATER. ZEE LOOKED EVERYWHERE FOR ELIJAH. BUT HE WAS NOWHERE to be found. When she got on the bus at the end of the day, she took her seat only after searching to make sure he wasn't on there already. As the bus rumbled to life and started to pull out of the parking lot, someone slipped into the seat next to Zee, snapping her out of her thoughts.

It was Nellie.

"What do you want?" Zee said, turning back to the window.

"I want you to stop this."

"Stop what?"

Nellie rolled her eyes. "You know what I'm talking about. The new principal knows."

"Knows what?"

"About you attacking me."

Zee scowled. "You started it. And you don't know for sure that that's what he's talking about."

Nellie touched her nose self-consciously. It was still bandaged, and for a moment, Zee felt bad. But then she pushed that feeling down into her toes, where it couldn't bother her anymore.

"He *was* talking about us and you know it," Nellie said. "This is all your fault."

"Maybe you should have thought of that before you opened your mouth and said all those lies that you said. Or before you called me Ghost Girl or Zero. Why don't you just go back to your perfect little life with your perfect parents and your perfect house and leave me alone?"

Zee elbowed past her and got off the bus at Elijah's stop. She needed to talk to her friend. Her *only* friend.

She jogged down the shoulder of the road, around the bend, and up the driveway of Elijah's house. She bounded up the steps and was about to knock on the door when she heard muffled shouting. She froze, fist hovering in the air. She wasn't sure what to do. Inside, muffled voices rose in waves. A bit afraid, she backed up to go home, when the porch door swung open and Elijah came out.

Startled to see her, he swiped quickly at the tears on his face. "Zee," he said, "what are you doing here?"

"I just . . ." Zee forced a smile. "I wanted to talk to you about the new principal. I saw you go up there! That was crazy!"

The porch door opened, and Elijah's father stood there, filling the doorway. "Oh, hello, Zee."

"Hello, sir."

"You forgot the trash." He handed the bag to Elijah. "Be sure to lock the lid, okay? Last time the raccoons got in," he said. Then with a snorting laugh he added, "Not that there's much left in there, considering your healthy appetite!"

Zee didn't dare look Elijah in the eye. His father ruffled his hair as if that offset his cruelty.

When Zee was younger, her father got into an argument with a neighbor who used a slur. He told her that whenever she saw that kind of behavior, she should always say something. That she should never let another person be degraded and humiliated without speaking up, including speaking up for herself. "Words have power," her father said, his hazel eyes meeting hers. "Never forget that, Zee. Words can destroy and they can save, so choose them carefully.

They are the most powerful weapon you can yield."

She had gone to bed feeling good, sure her father was some kind of superhero. But her dad wasn't here now. No one was here now except for her and Elijah, doing his best not to let the tears fall, and his father, acting like it was no big deal to make his own son feel terrible. Elijah's father had always said things that hurt his son, but this felt so much bigger. It felt outright cruel. It felt like the kind of thinking that Principal Scratch talked about. The kind that put your own desires ahead of people you are supposed to love and protect. She should say something. Her father taught her to stand up for herself and others, but Mr. Turner was a grown-up. And he was big. Really big. In front of him she felt so small. Telling grown-ups they were wrong seemed impossible. And all the good words that she knew felt lodged in her throat.

The door slammed shut as Mr. Turner went back in.

Elijah grabbed the bag and dragged it to the metal trash cans at the side of the house. He pulled the cans to the end of the long driveway, and Zee followed him wordlessly.

There were a few minutes of awkward silence. Zee thought about asking him if he was okay, but her words still felt stuck in her throat. That happened sometimes. If she had a story to tell, her words flowed like water, but when she had to be honest, or do something that scared her or made her feel vulnerable, it was like her mouth was full of dry rocks. Her tongue couldn't seem to form the words.

Instead, Elijah spoke first. "What are you doing here?"

"I just . . ." She cleared her throat. Why did he sound mad at her? What did she do? "The assembly? What happened in assembly? What made you go up there?"

"I . . . I don't know. It was so strange; it was like I couldn't stop myself. When he asked if someone would come up, it was like a voice inside me said I had to do this. I had to stand up for myself. I just felt like for a second that maybe he was right. What if there was something going on with my dad that was . . . wrong? Something that needed to be addressed. Something I needed to say out loud."

Zee started to laugh but then stopped when she looked at her friend's face.

"All that talk about bullies and standing up for yourself when no one will. For a minute I felt like it might work—like if I said it out loud, I could do something about it—which is stupid, I know."

Zee stared at the ground. There were those rocks

again. She forced her tongue around them. "No, I don't think it's stupid."

"It's just my dad . . ." For a moment, Elijah looked like he was going to cry, but then he turned angry. "He always brings up my weight. I just think he . . . would like me better if I weighed less. If I were into sports like he is."

"Don't say that," Zee said, just above a whisper. "You're amazing, smart, and—"

"No, he would. He used to be heavy like me, but then he lost weight and worked out and got popular. If I were in better shape, maybe I could play sports. He wants a son that plays football, not one that gets good grades and loves science and wanders through cemeteries."

The smallest ripple passed over Zee's face and then was gone.

"No offense," Elijah added, half-heartedly.

Zee cleared her throat. "None taken." It was an easy lie.

"I thought if Principal Scratch could somehow understand . . ." Elijah trailed off. "And he did, Zee."

"What?" Zee pressed. The silence between them was filled with the low chatter of crickets.

"After the assembly, he stopped me in the hall and I went to his office and we talked about my dad."

"What did he say?"

"He asked me why I said my father was my bully. And I told him it was 'cause he wanted me to be like him. He wanted me to be athletic and active and . . . well, not me. But then Principal Scratch asked me why I wasn't doing that. He wanted to know why I didn't want to make my father happy."

"What?" Zee said. "He actually said that?"

"Yeah. He said that I should try harder and do better and not let my father down. He said that I could be the son my dad wants. That it would be better for me. He said he believed in me."

"Is that what you want?" Zee asked softly.

"I don't know. Maybe he's right. I don't want to let my father down."

"Maybe your father is letting *you* down, Elijah."

"That's not how it works, Zee. I want him to be proud of me. Maybe if he was, then my mother . . ." Elijah paused, swallowed some words, and blurted, "I just thought it would fix things, okay? It's stupid, I know."

"But, Elijah, you're smart and kind and good at everything you do. That's what I see when I look at you. There's so much more to you than what you weigh."

"Don't do that!" Elijah said loudly. "You always

do that and I hate it. Don't tell me that I'm not fat, okay? I am. I have eyes."

"I'm sorry," Zee whispered, startled by his yelling. Elijah didn't yell. He just wasn't built like that. And the fact that Zee of all people had brought him to this point, well, it said something. She felt awful. She just wanted this conversation to end. Wanted to go back to talking about their usual stuff like school and how she was going to get back at Nellie Bloom. Not this kind of talk. Not the kind that twisted her stomach and dried up her mouth.

"Most days I don't even care, you know? Most days it doesn't matter, but there are times when he looks at me . . ." Elijah looked back at the house. "He looks at me like . . . he just sees a lifetime of unhappiness. Even though I'm not unhappy." Elijah sighed. "I just . . . I don't know. I want my father to be proud of me. I think I want that more than anything. More than even being myself."

Zee chewed on the inside of her lip. This didn't sound like Elijah. Suddenly she hated Principal Scratch for getting in his head like this. "Well, if you ask me, you're the only interesting person in this whole stupid town. That's the only thing that matters to me. Who cares what your dad thinks?"

"I do! That's the whole point, Zee," Elijah snapped. His words were icy, and he turned his back on her. "Are you even listening?"

Zee flinched. It wasn't the first time someone had asked her that. She took a deep breath. "Elijah . . . this isn't you. This is *him*. You don't need to change. You don't need to be thinner. It won't change a single thing about you. Fathers are supposed to love you no matter what. They shouldn't want to change you."

Elijah looked up at Zee, and she could see the tears in his eyes. "Yeah, but . . . what if he does want me to change? What do I do then?"

Zee opened her mouth and then closed it again. "I don't know, but that new principal isn't going to fix it. Also, what's the story with that red hand? It freaks me out," Zee said with a small smile. She nudged his arm, and something like a smile flickered over his face. "Look, maybe your dad doesn't realize that it hurts you. Sometimes parents mess up and don't do a good job being parents. Look at my dad."

"He's just looking for work," Elijah offered.

Zee kicked at the stones near her feet. "He's been gone for a long time. It's irresponsible. Abby . . . she's trying to stay positive, but what if what Nellie said was right?"

"Nellie Bloom is a bossy little know-it-all. Your dad will be home soon," Elijah said, putting an arm around Zee's shoulder.

"Speaking of Nellie," Zee said, feeling like the conversation was tipping back into a space she could navigate. "We have a lot of work ahead of us. I need you in top scheming mode."

"What now?" Elijah said, and the beginnings of a smile crept across his face.

"Revenge," Zee said, offering him a smile as wide and wicked as they come.

7

A SECOND STORM FOLLOWED THAT NIGHT. NOT AS BIG AS THE FIRST
one, but rain still lashed at Zee's window, pulling her
right out of her dreams. She sat up in bed, trying to
remember the strange dream that now burned off in
a haze. She couldn't put her finger on exactly what
happened, but she was sure of one thing—a cold in
her belly sort of feeling. The same feeling she had at
the library right before she saw Paul. She shivered and
pulled the blankets up around her as she climbed out
of bed and went to the window. The rain was coming
in torrents, the wind carrying it in all different direc-
tions so that it was hard to see anything. Zee hoisted
the blanket up over her shoulders, cupped her hands

to the window, and peered into the darkness.

A blast of lightning lit up the sky, startling her. The street was aglow for just a second before it went dark again. But it was long enough for Zee to see *something* on the sidewalk in front of her house. It was a shadow, a thing standing perfectly still.

The sky cracked with thunder that Zee felt down in her bones. The first storm was thrilling. This one felt different. Colder. Deeper.

Haunted.

When the lightning lit up her street again, she saw the figure. She was sure of it. A stock-still gray mass staring up at her house. Who could stand out there in this weather? Her heart thudded inside her chest. Should she get Abby? Zee glanced back at her alarm clock. It was 3:00 a.m. exactly.

The witching hour. She'd read about it in a book. The time, they say, that witches are at their most powerful. A time when strange things could happen.

Abby worked a double yesterday and would need to get up soon for her next shift. It was wrong to wake her up. Especially over something so silly. Zee squinted again. It had to be a shadow, a trick of the light, a post office box she'd never noticed before. Something other than whatever that cold flush in her belly was telling her it was.

When lightning hit again, followed by a peal of thunder—a sign that the storm was moving closer—she gasped because this time she saw it clearly.

Sitting on the sidewalk was the hound she'd seen in the cemetery. It sat there patiently and calmly—the thing didn't even look wet—and it stared up at her window. She could see the faint glint of its red eyes.

And then she heard it.

A voice. Deep and raspy but clear.

"Hoooowwww much looooonnnggggggeeerrrr?"

Zee spun around—it sounded like it was behind her—her eyes darted from door to bed to nightstand to dresser to closet back to door. Her heart rammed against her ribs. The room was empty.

She squeezed her fingers to try to stop the shaking. When she turned back to the window, the next blast of lightning revealed . . . nothing. Had she been wrong? The sidewalk was empty.

But that voice. That question—"How much longer?"—burned inside her. She'd heard it clear as day. It wasn't the kind of thing she'd imagined. Or was it?

She squeezed her eyes shut. *Go back to bed. This is probably just a really bad dream.*

Zee picked up her water glass off the nightstand. Empty. Her throat was dry. She felt an overwhelming need to go downstairs and check to make sure the front door was locked. She squeezed the glass in her hand, trying to stop the shaking. She was going to get water, check the lock, and then go back to sleep.

As she left her room and climbed down the steps, she thought, *You used to be scared of nothing. What's happened?*

She crossed the living room, jumping as another blast of lightning lit up the room. She got to the kitchen and turned on the faucet, refilling her glass, which she gulped down followed by another. She double-checked to make sure the door was locked, pulling on the handle until it rattled.

She carried her water glass through the living room as thunder rattled the window and another burst of lightning lit up the living room as if someone had turned on the lights. And that was when she saw it.

Eyes, wide and white and shining, and then a mouth, open. Long ragged hair. Mud-stained face.

A woman, caked in wet mud and moss, was huddled near the arm of the couch staring at Zee.

The water glass clattered to the floor, and Zee screamed and screamed and screamed, unable to stop herself. She was sure she was going to scream forever, until her throat went raw and cracked open.

Abby's bedroom door flew open, and she raced down the steps and flipped on the lights. She crouched down and pulled her sister into a hug. "Calm down, Zee, everything's fine." Abby shushed her and rocked her until she was breathing normally again. Zee stared at the empty space at the edge of the couch. What had she seen?

"What happened?" Abby whispered into her hair. "What are you doing down here?"

"Water," Zee managed to croak. "I needed some water."

For a second, she wanted to tell Abby everything. About the hound outside and the woman in the living room, but it started to feel just like a crazy dream. A vivid one, but a dream nonetheless. Something her imagination conjured up. Another bolt of lightning lit up the window, followed by the rumble of thunder.

"It's all these storms," Abby said. "They're unnerving. Let's get you back into bed."

Zee nodded. It was the most she could do. Her sister scooped up the glass and swept into the kitchen to refill it before taking her sister's hand and walking her back upstairs. Once she was back in bed, she started to feel like she could breathe again. It was just that overactive imagination of hers. At least that was what she kept telling herself.

"You want me to leave the light on?" Abby asked.

"No, it's okay," Zee said, scooting back under the

covers. "It was just a trick of the light or something."

"Okay. I love you, Zee. Get some sleep," Abby said, and got up, turned out the light, and closed the door. Zee breathed a few times, listening to the sounds of the house settling and the wind and rain at the window. She inhaled long through her nose and exhaled through her mouth just like her father taught her when she felt the panic clawing its way up her throat.

Inhale. Exhale.

Longer inhale. Longer exhale.

Zee felt her heart start to settle as she pulled the covers up around her head and hugged her pillow tight. *There was nothing there. It was just your imagination.*

Inhale. Exhale.

Just your imagination.

Inhale. Exhale.

She heard it then. The steady creak of the steps. *It's just Abby,* she told herself. But she didn't believe it. Whatever was coming down the hall had wet, thunking steps; it shuffled, as if it were dragging itself toward her bedroom door.

Zee's long, smooth breaths sped up as the panic ratcheted up her spine, causing her arms and legs to feel stiff. Each breath was coming faster and faster as fear made the air catch and snag in her lungs. She was freezing. She saw her breath mist in the air. She stared at her door, afraid to blink because she was certain that it was about to slowly creak open and from the hall she would see it.

Mud-ruined long hair.

Wide eyes, all white.

Zee squeezed her eyes shut. She wanted to call for Abby, but she couldn't get the words out. Zee pulled the blanket over her head and willed it all to stop.

8

ZEE WOKE WITH A START WHEN HER SISTER OPENED THE DOOR.

"Time to get up, lazybones," Abby said before heading back down the staircase.

Zee poked her head out from under the covers and squinted in the morning light. The door to her bedroom was open; she could hear Abby banging around the kitchen downstairs. The storm had passed, and sunlight spilled into her room, turning it back into a safe place, lighting up her nightstand and the bookcase in the corner and the hammock chair her father made for her. All of it was awash in bright sunlight, sweeping away the night and with it the memory of the terrifying woman. An image that had burned so bright last night revealed itself to be nothing in the morning light.

Now that *was a nightmare,* she thought, tossing the covers back. She pulled herself out of bed, the floorboards cold on her bare feet, and got dressed. As she headed down the hall, she stopped. She should be going into the bathroom, washing her face, brushing her hair, and then heading down for breakfast, but she couldn't move. Along the floorboards was a streak of brown and green.

She touched it with her finger, then picked some up and sniffed it.

Mud and moss.

She glanced back into her room at her boots on the floor. Her heart tripped inside her.

This is not what it looks like, she thought. *This is just a coincidence.* She picked up her boot and found some small tracing of mud from the other day. With a bit of relief, Zee reasoned that the mud just got on the hallway floor because she wasn't being careful. That's all. Nothing weird happening here. She swallowed, her throat tight, and headed downstairs and into the kitchen.

"Your lunch is packed and in your bag. That's breakfast," Abby said, motioning at the cereal on the kitchen counter. Zee pulled the stool out and tucked into the bowl. "By the way, I saw that math test you shoved into the bottom of your bag."

Zee groaned. She had forgotten about failing that test. Forgotten on purpose, hence shoving it to the bottom of her backpack.

"Do we need a tutor?"

"No," she said, spooning cereal into her mouth. "I just forgot about the quiz, so I didn't study and . . ."

"We can't have you failing math, Zee. You're too bright to be failing things. I need you to make time to study. Where is that calendar I bought you? You were supposed to put all your quizzes on there so you could be prepared."

"It's not a big deal, Abby," Zee said.

"Failing is a big deal, Zee."

"It won't happen again."

Abby gave her sister a look and then poured herself more coffee. "Did you get back to sleep?"

Zee froze her spoon midway to her mouth. "What . . . what do you mean?"

"After your nightmare? Did you get back to sleep?"

Zee's belly flushed cold again, and the image of the woman's face floated up. "Yeah," she said, squeezing her eyes shut. "I got back to sleep. Sorry about that."

"Nothing to be sorry about. Like I said last night, with all these storms we've been having it makes the whole town feel haunted. Like those storms keep washing up ghosts."

In her mind, Zee saw that hound at her window. She heard the voice again—the long, low echoing question that haunted her. She shivered, unable to stop herself. She thought for a moment about telling Abby everything. About the hound, about the question of how much longer, and the woman she saw crouched at the arm of the couch, but the words felt like rocks. Instead she shoveled in more cereal, chewing slowly.

Later at school, Zee spent her lunch hour sitting on the ledge near the small patchy bit of grass that her school considered a lawn, reading.

"You're reading that book again?" Elijah said, dropping his book bag onto the grass. "How many times is it?"

Zee slipped her bookmark into her very worn copy of *Frankenstein*. The cover had fallen off a while ago, and she'd used duct tape to reattach it and reinforce the spine. The first few pages were loose, so she was always really careful with them. There was water damage from the time Abby knocked over her drink while the book was on the table, so some of the pages were stiff and warped.

"Why don't you get a new copy?" Elijah asked, opening up the foil that held his sandwich.

"I don't want a new copy. I like this copy," Zee said, laying a protective hand over the book.

"No, but seriously, how many times have you read it?" Elijah asked.

"I don't know," Zee said, her mouth full of bagel. "Probably a dozen or so."

"Man, all those stories out there and you just keep on reading the same ones."

"I like it. It's interesting. You know Mary Shelley was only eighteen when she came up with this story. A monster made from the dead. It's incredible."

Even as she said the words, the face of the woman crouched by the couch last night flashed behind Zee's eyelids and goose bumps raced up her arms.

"How did she come up with it?" Elijah asked.

"She was at Lake Geneva in Switzerland with Lord Byron and her boyfriend Percy. Byron challenged each of them to write a story. I don't know what the others wrote about. But at the time there was a scientist trying to reanimate a dead frog. She had seen the illustrations in the newspaper. That night when she went to sleep she saw it. A man, stitched together from the body parts of the dead. Another man, desperate to bring him to life. So Mary Shelley wrote about a monster and the creator who rejected him."

"Bolts in the neck, right?" Elijah said.

"No, that's just the movie. Her book isn't like that at all. It's really good. Come on, the woman literally invented science fiction."

There was something else Zee liked about Mary Shelley that she didn't tell Elijah. Something she didn't tell anyone. Mary was attracted to the dark, just like Zee. Mary was a great writer like Zee hoped to be. She was also an incredible storyteller. But they had something else—something even more important—in common. Something Zee could only whisper to herself.

"So, something happened last night," Zee said, picking at her fingernails instead of looking at Elijah.

"Okay."

"I . . . um, during the storm, I woke up and looked outside and saw the wolf, er . . . the dog."

Elijah cocked a speculative eyebrow. "Like the one you saw in the cemetery?" he asked.

"Yeah."

"Go on."

"And um, it was just sitting outside my house. Just sitting there in all that rain and wind. Looking up at my window."

"What're you going to call this story?" Elijah said.

"It's not a story, Elijah. It happened."

"Okay," he said, but Zee could tell he didn't believe her.

"You have to believe me. The dog . . . hound . . . whatever it is . . . was there. Sitting right on the sidewalk in the storm staring up at my window. And it . . . spoke."

Elijah choked on his water. He started to laugh. "The *dog* spoke to you."

"Yeah. It said, 'How much longer?'"

"You heard the dog speak to you all the way up on the second floor during a storm. This is a far-fetched story even for you, Zee."

"The voice was in my room. Sort of all around me at once. But I know it was from the hound. I heard it clear as day. It dragged the words out, like 'Howwwww much looonnngggeeeerrrr?'"

"Okay, stop, that's creepy."

"Elijah, I'm not telling you a story. This really happened."

"Maybe it was a dream," he offered nervously. "It sounds like you might have had a really bad dream. I heard about these things called night terrors. Maybe it was one of those."

"It wasn't a dream. It happened. And there's more. After I heard the voice, the dog vanished. I went downstairs to get a glass of water, and there was . . . a woman in my living room at the end of my couch. She was sort of crouched down."

"Okay, I don't like this story. Stop."

"Elijah," she said, grabbing his hand. It felt so warm; Zee just now realized how cold she was. "It happened. She was there. She was covered in mud and moss, and it was like she was screaming but there was no sound."

"Stop," Elijah said, closing his eyes and holding up a hand.

"And then after I went back upstairs, I heard something shuffling down the hall. Sort of these wet stumbling footsteps. And then I could have sworn my door creaked open, but I put the covers over my head and—"

"I said stop." Elijah looked sick. He looked the way Zee imagined she looked last night.

"She was in the hall. I know she was. I saw a ghost, Elijah. I swear I'm not making this up."

He stood. "Stop it right now. This isn't a funny story."

"It's not a story!"

He gave her a look. "You're telling me this really happened last night. All of it?"

"Yes."

"You swear?"

"Yes."

"Pinkie swear?" he said, putting his finger out.

Zee hooked hers to his. "Pinkie swear."

The bell rang, and everyone started filing back into the building.

He still looked unsure as he picked his backpack up off the ground and added, "If you're telling the truth, and I'm guessing you are, then you have to tell Abby because this is serious, Zee."

She knew he expected her to balk. To take it back. But instead she said, "Fine. We'll tell Abby. You come over my house after school today. I'll tell her the exact same story I told you."

Zee was happy to see that Abby was already home when they got there, which meant she hadn't worked a double shift. Elijah and Zee dropped their backpacks on the floor and headed into the kitchen.

"Hello," Abby said, kissing the top of Zee's head as she passed. "Hello, Elijah."

"Hi, Abby," he said with a shy smile.

"How was school today? No fighting, right?" She side-eyed her sister.

"I need to talk to you, Abby," Zee said.

"Oh no, what now?"

"It's about last night." Zee took a breath, then exchanged a look with Elijah. "The thing that woke me up wasn't a dream. And what I saw wasn't a trick of the light." She told the whole story. The storm. The dog. The voice. The whole time Abby went about her business in the kitchen putting together a snack for Zee and Elijah. She nodded and said "uh-huh" where it was appropriate as she cut up carrots and set out pita chips and hummus.

"It was just a pair of eyes at first, and then a mouth," Zee said. "It was a woman in our living room. She was covered in mud and moss and it was like she was screaming but there was no sound. My belly felt like it was full of ice; I could barely breathe it was so cold."

Abby dropped the water glass in her hand. It shattered on the floor; water, ice cubes, and shards of glass went flying.

"Whoa, Abby, you okay?" Elijah said.

But Abby just looked at Zee, her hand over her mouth, and in a breathy whisper she said, "What do you mean cold?"

"Cold. Like I swallowed ice cubes. My whole insides went freezing. It happened at the library too."

"At the library? What happened at the library?"

"I was in the stacks, looking for a book, and I just

felt this terrible cold, like I stepped into a freezer, and suddenly there was this boy there. He said his name was Paul and he worked there. Then he just vanished."

"You have it."

"What?" Zee said, genuinely afraid of her sister's reaction. Abby was white as a sheet as she tried to sweep up the glass shards. Zee watched her, and how her hands were shaking. She couldn't clean the glass, so after a minute of trying, she just sat down at the counter next to them. Abby was always levelheaded and logical, and the way she looked now brought that sick feeling into Zee's belly.

"You have it too," Abby repeated.

"What?"

"She could communicate with the . . . dead. Mostly she would just talk to them. Listen to their stories."

The cold flush spread into Zee's chest. She wanted Abby to stop talking. Her sister was supposed to refute this. She was supposed to find a logical simple explanation. She wasn't supposed to sit across from her at the table and tell her that she was the one thing she didn't want to be.

Haunted.

"Wait," Elijah said, interrupting Abby. "Who are we talking about?"

Abby's and Zee's gaze met across the counter.

She knew. She knew the minute Abby dropped that glass on the floor. In some ways, maybe she'd always known.

Still, when the words came out of Abby's mouth, they felt like a gut punch. Not because she was surprised, but because it was a word they rarely said anymore. A word they danced around. A word that was itself haunted.

"Our mother."

Later that night, after Elijah went home, Zee was upstairs in her bedroom, reading *Frankenstein*, when her sister knocked on the door. Abby came and sat on the edge of Zee's bed. "You feeling okay?"

It seemed like a strange question to ask. How could she be okay? Her mother could talk to ghosts. So could Zee, apparently. And now one of them, a terrifying one, had found its way into her home. Every time she looked at the couch, she could see those wide eyes. That mouth twisted in a silent scream.

And then she thought about Paul in the library. The way he seemed off. The way he seemed familiar to her. The way no one else could see him. But Paul was nice. Sweet. This woman, whoever she was, terrified her.

"Look," Abby said, "I know what happened to you last night was scary and I know it's a lot to ingest, but Mom loved her gift. She felt blessed by it. She really found joy in helping these people through their transition."

"I just want to know who she is and why she's in our house."

"I'm sure she does too. Mom used to say some ghosts got confused. She said they could either forget their old life or remember it too much."

"But Paul didn't feel stuck or confused."

Abby shrugged. "See? They're not all scary."

"But this woman is scary, Abby."

"I know, but she won't hurt you."

"You don't know that."

"Mom always said—"

"But Mom isn't here," Zee said. She wondered how long it had been since she'd actually said the M-word. It was such a tiny word, one little syllable, but it was big enough to crack open her heart. A word so small that meant so very much. Abby reached up and smoothed back her hair.

"I know. I miss her too."

I don't even know what to miss, Zee thought. She didn't know anything about her mother, really. She knew dumb things. That she liked winter better than summer. That she liked to tell stories too. That her favorite ice cream flavor was coffee. That she always wanted to travel but was terrified of flying. That she went overboard when it came to decorating the house for Christmas. She knew that her mother was born in Scotland, and she never lost her accent. She knew she loved tacos. But these things didn't add up to a person. They were just facts stacked side by side. She didn't know what her mother's voice sounded like or how she smelled. Or what it would feel like when she kissed Zee on the top of the head, or absentmindedly played with her hair. She didn't know what face she would have made when Zee was in trouble. What she looked like when she laughed. She didn't even know what her laugh sounded like. She'd imagined a thousand and one conversations with her mother, but none of them were true.

"She loved you so much, Zee. She couldn't wait for you to be born. She had your name picked out—without Dad's help, mind you—the second she found out she was pregnant. You know why she named you Zera?"

Zee swallowed hard. She did know, but there was something comforting in listening to Abby tell her again. It was the same story she'd been telling her since she was a little girl. It felt like a line that could stretch back through time. Something that could tether her to her mother when nothing else did.

"First she wanted to give you a name that no one else ever had. She heard it in a dream the day before she found out she was pregnant. She said that the name"—Abby smoothed back Zee's hair—"was a gift from the universe. Just like you. And she said with the two of us she now had her Abby to Zera. Her A to Z. Her family was complete, and her heart was full."

Zee bit down hard on her cheek as her throat went tight. She tried to stop the tears that pricked at her eyes.

"I think it's wonderful that you have this gift from her. It was so important to her, Zee. She used it to help people. I know you'll do the same. When you were born, with that full head of white hair, she took one look at you and said, 'I've known you all my life.' She wanted you more than she wanted anything in the world."

More than she wanted to be alive? Zee wondered but didn't say.

"I know this all seems strange and scary. But sometimes scary and strange is good. Mom always used to talk to me about taking risks. 'Never want perfection,' she would tell me. 'Be happy to fail because at least you tried something new.'

"Besides," Abby continued, "just because something is unfamiliar doesn't mean it's bad. I can't imagine how you're feeling but . . . I wish she were here." Abby paused, composed herself, and went on, "She would know what to say. She would know how to help you learn how to help them. I'm not like you or her. I don't know . . ." She trailed off and then said, "The only advice I can give you is to try to talk to your ghosts. Speak to them. Be a light for them. Talk to your ghost, Zee. Help her."

But Zee didn't want a ghost. She didn't want any of this.

"You look beat," Abby said, kissing her cheek. "Don't stay up too late reading that book." She pointed at *Frankenstein*. "I love you."

"I love you too," Zee said. "Hey, Abby?"

"Yes?" she said from the doorway.

"Have you heard from Dad?"

"I tried him earlier today, but it went to voice mail."

"Okay."

"I'm sure he's fine. Just busy. Get some sleep."

Her sister left the door open a crack.

Zee thought about what Nellie Bloom had said. What if Dad really had left them for good? What if it was just her and Abby now? She turned over the book and looked at the picture of Mary Shelley on the back. She thought about all the ways they were alike. Both storytellers drawn to darkness. She wondered if Mary Shelley saw ghosts too.

They certainly had something else in common. Another, bigger thing. One she wouldn't talk to Elijah or Abby or anyone else about. It was simple: Mary Shelley's mother, Mary Wollstonecraft, died giving birth to her.

Just like Zee's mom.

Mary didn't look like a killer. Zee wondered if that was true about her too? It's easy to be told something isn't your fault. That it was an accident. An unfortunate infection. But it's much harder to believe that to be true. Zee was here. Her mother was not. If Zee had not been born, her mother would still be alive. It was as if only one of them could exist at a time.

They were opposite sides of a coin. No matter how many times it was flipped, one of them would be here and the other would not. Zee and her mother could never be together. No matter what. And now she had this thing she shared with her mom—this ability— except her mom would never be able to talk to her about it, to explain it to her. It just wasn't fair.

She studied the picture again. Did Mary feel guilty

too? Was she sad? Did she also ache for this person she never got to know?

Zee thought about how great it felt when her foot made contact with Nellie's face and the blood went everywhere. She thought about how she lost . . . maybe even . . . killed . . . her own mother.

Maybe that was all she was good for—hurting people.

Maybe that's why the dogs were at her window and the ghosts gathered in her home.

Maybe Zera Delilah Puckett just had to be more of the type of person Principal Scratch told them about. Did she think about herself enough? About what she wanted? Principal Scratch told Elijah he should be better for his father. Should she change too?

THE NEXT MORNING. WHILE ZEE WAS GETTING READY FOR SCHOOL.
there was a knock on the front door. She leaned out
her bedroom, one sneaker on, and heard her sister
open the front door.

"Oh! I . . . Of course, no, no trouble at all . . . Please
come in," she heard her sister say. "I'm so happy to
meet you. Can I get you anything . . . ?"

Then another voice, a low baritone murmur that
Zee felt in her bones.

"Yes, of course," her sister said. "Let me get
her. . . . Zee! Can you come down here?"

Not liking the sound of this, Zee slipped on her

other shoe, tied her shoelaces, and headed down the stairs. She worried it was her math teacher about the failed quiz. Or worse, the guidance counselor, Mr. Jacobs. He was constantly stopping kids in the hall to talk about their feelings. Like school wasn't a war zone. Like every day wasn't a battle to just get through without grown-ups adding extra trouble.

When Zee got to the bottom of the stairs, she saw Principal Scratch. He was dressed in a long-sleeved black button-down shirt and black pants. His hair looked slick with oil. He was staring out the front window, hands clasped behind his back. He was a tableau of black except for the splash of red from his glove. Seeing him there made her heart stutter.

"Mr. Scratch," Abby said, "this is my sister, Zee."

He turned around, still wearing those sunglasses, and smiled a wide, bright smile at Zee. He took the glasses off, and his eyes had a mischievous glint about them. "Pleasure to officially meet you, Zee," he said, his voice satin smooth. He reached out that red-gloved hand, but Zee didn't want to shake it. She chanced a look at her sister, hoping for some backup, but instead, Abby widened her eyes at Zee, a sure sign that she had to *behave*. Tentatively, Zee shook his hand. The glove was strangely cold and smooth. It didn't feel like fabric wrapped around a human hand, but more like porcelain, or rubber. "Though I do know you by reputation already."

Abby frowned as Principal Scratch continued, "Your sister and I were just having a little chat. I hope you were able to make it to the assembly the other day."

Zee nodded.

"Good. I hope you found my thoughts on bullying and *fighting* helpful." He cocked a sharp eyebrow and then cleared his throat and said, "Since I'm the new principal I wanted to take a moment to get to know my students and their families. I wanted to make sure everything was good," he said, sitting in the nearby armchair. He motioned for Zee and Abby to also sit down. "Anything you might want to talk to me about, Zee?"

Zee shook her head.

"Are we sure?"

Abby was staring daggers at Zee, but she knew it was better to feign ignorance than confess outright.

Principal Scratch sighed. "Well, I do know you've been having some trouble in school lately, Zee."

Zee scowled. Did Nellie tell? No, it was probably Mr. Houston.

"N-n-n-nothing big, really," she stammered.

"Oh, no?" Principal Scratch cocked an eyebrow. "Failing your math test and fighting with fellow students. Yes, I know all about it. You're in what, sixth grade?"

"Yes, sir."

"Hmmmm, yes, difficult time. Not quite a child anymore. Not quite a teenager. Just a strange in-between time. A vulnerable time. In the school, we joke that it is a testing time. But not just those types of tests. It's a time when we walk that delicate line between good and bad. Between bully and friend. Remember what I said about standing up for yourself?"

Zee bowed her head, thinking about the other day and how good it felt to kick Nellie Bloom in the face. "Stand for you."

He chuckled softly. "That's right. It's just a rather good saying, don't you think? About this transition—the not-a-child-not-a-teenager-yet—this time is difficult. Abby knows what I'm talking about. Right, Abby?"

"Um . . . sure," Abby said and nodded, but the sisters exchanged a small conspiratorial look. Zee was quite sure that Abby thought Principal Scratch was just as loony as she did.

"And this time is always harder on girls than it is

on boys. History is full of stories. Look at the Salem witch trials, the danger those girls courted . . ."

"I'm not courting anything," Zee said loudly. *What did that even mean? "Look at the Salem witch trials"?* Sometimes it seemed like women could be killed for just existing.

Principal Scratch chuckled. "So much energy. So much *life*. That's the thing I love so much about teaching young people. You could feed off their energy. Just snack on it." He licked his lips and turned toward Abby. "Now then, is your mother home?"

Zee dropped her eyes, anger stirring inside her.

"She passed away, sir," Abby said. "Eleven years ago."

"Oh! I'm so sorry. How sad," Principal Scratch said, but there was something weird about the way he said it. Like he already knew the answer before he'd asked the question. "A pity you never got to meet your mother and she you . . . what a sacrifice."

Zee stared at the floor, anger burning inside her. She couldn't even look at him.

"And how old are you, Abby?"

"Twenty-one, sir."

"My, that was a lot for you to manage at such a young age. That must be quite the struggle for you both. Zee, have you talked to anyone about this? The guidance counselor, Mr. Jacobs, is unfortunately no longer at the school. I, sadly, had to do a bit of house-cleaning when I started. But my door is always open, Zee. Sometimes we just need the right drive, you know? We need to find the thing we want the most and focus everything on that. Just really dig in and make it happen for ourselves, because we must act for ourselves. I am happy to work through these feelings with you. Really get to the root of it all. Figure out what you want for *you*."

"N . . . no," Zee stammered. She felt her cheeks go red. She really wanted Scratch, as she now thought of him, to leave.

He looked at Abby. "Something to think about, Abby. My door is open for you too, but especially for Zee. She's in a very vulnerable place. Very vulnerable. Could be at the root of the falling grades and fight-ing."

The way he turned his eyes on her made her shiver. "It's not . . . I didn't. Nellie Bloom started it!"

"Of course, Zee," he said, reaching over and pat-ting her knee with that red hand. "Your sister and I are just concerned for you. We want to make sure you're safe and not just surviving but thriving, as we like to say. Right, Abby? We want you to figure out what you want and to reach out and take it."

"Of course," Abby said, but she didn't meet her sister's eyes.

"And your father?"

"He's upstate looking for work," Abby said. "He heard about a construction opportunity a couple counties away. The pay was good."

"When did he leave?"

"Nearly six months ago."

Zee balked. Six months? Had it *already* been six months?

"So," Principal Scratch said, "it's just the two of you? That is a lot to have on your plate, Abigail."

"We're managing, sir. Lots of others have it much harder."

"Others have it harder," Scratch repeated, holding up his hands. "That is so generous of you, Abby, but you must miss him."

"We do," Abby said, taking her sister's hand. "We haven't heard from him in a while, and I have been a touch worried. I know the area he's working in might have bad cell service. I just wish he would find some way to check in. Some way to let us know he's okay." Abby's voice faltered, and Zee feared she was going to cry. She didn't want Abby to do that in front of Principal Scratch. But she also didn't want Abby to do that in front of *her*. She knew that was unfair, but it was still true. Zee wasn't sure how to comfort her sister, and if Abby lost hope, then Zee would lose hope too. Then they would have nothing left.

Principal Scratch leaned forward. "Hmm, you must want to hear from him. You must want that more than anything else in the world right now?"

Abby nodded and swallowed hard. She cleared her throat and said, "But I know my father. He's doing his best and I believe in him. I know he'll be back soon."

"Have you tried guided meditation? Visualization practices? It really helps to clear the mind and focus on what needs to happen next. It can be life-changing. The basic principle is to see yourself in your mind's eye obtaining what you desire most. You must always focus on what you want, on your deepest desires. The world can be a difficult place, and people can just get swallowed up. You have to learn how to put your needs first; then, and only then, do you have a fighting chance. Once you focus on those needs, those desires, you can get everything you want out of life. It's like a key that opens the door to power. Something, I imagine, that you, Abby, feel like you don't have."

Principal Scratch stood. "Well, I won't take up too much more of your time. I know Zee needs to get to school and you're off to work. So all I'm going to say is this." Scratch reached out with that red glove and squeezed Abby's shoulders. Zee couldn't help but see that she sort of relaxed into his touch. Like she'd been waiting all this time for someone else to be in charge. "I am very committed to helping people find their power. To helping them get everything they want in life. Let me guide you. Because you deserve it, Abigail. I hope you don't mind me saying, but I checked your file and I know you . . . well, circumstances obviously changed your path, but I hope you will think about talking with me. My door is always open."

Principal Scratch put his sunglasses back on and said, "And remember what I said about focusing on yourself. It's your turn, Abby, after already having given up so much." He glanced briefly at Zee, and she bristled. Was he talking about her? "Remember, my door is always open. Now then, I must be going. Thank you for speaking with me. I find it's so helpful to get to know all my students and their families."

He turned to Zee and loomed over her. All she could see was her own warped face reflected in his wide shiny sunglasses. "And you. Behave for your sister. She has enough on her plate. Let's channel that feisty spirit into something a little more productive, yes? Let's spend some time figuring out what Zee wants most of all."

"I'll make sure she does, Principal Scratch," Abby said as they followed him into the kitchen and toward the front door. As he left, he passed by Abby's cell phone on the kitchen counter. He touched it just once with his gloved hand, the littlest tap, before looking back at her and saying, "Remember what I said about the power of visualization, about focusing on *your* hopes and dreams. Think about stopping by. There is much I can teach you."

Then he left. Once the door was shut and locked, Abby leaned against it, and the two of them started to laugh. "Well! That was just the weirdest—"

Her phone on the counter rang suddenly.

Abby picked it up, and Zee could see it was an unknown number.

"Hello," Abby said, and then she yelled, "Dad! Oh my goodness, Dad, it's so great to hear your voice. I've been trying to reach you." Abby was practically dancing around the kitchen with excitement.

Zee was excited too. She missed her father and couldn't wait till it was her turn to talk to him. But she couldn't shake the strange nagging feeling about Scratch's visit. The things he'd said. All the questions he'd asked about their family. The way he'd talked about the power of focusing on what you wanted most, the way he'd said he could give her power, then touched Abby's phone, and here, now, was her father on the line, the one person Abby wanted to talk to more than anyone in the world.

Ice filled Zee's belly. It just seemed a little too good to be true.

10

ZEE AND ELIJAH SPOTTED THE HANDMADE SIGNS ON THEIR WALK TO school. They were taped to the telephone pole offering a reward for the safe return of Max, a mixed-breed mini poodle, whose image was front and center on each flyer. The bottom of the flyer was cut into snippets with a phone number that could be torn off. There was a flyer on nearly every telephone pole, each bus shelter, and on the doors of most of the businesses.

"Someone really wants their dog back," Zee said as they passed another flyer. She thought of the hounds she'd seen and wondered if Max stood a chance against those creatures.

"Yeah, look who," Elijah said, pointing. Up the

street, Zee could see Nellie Bloom taping another flyer to a telephone pole.

A wicked smile tugged at Zee's lips. "Oh, brilliant," she said, her mind whirring.

"I don't like that look," Elijah said, his brow furrowed. "That's a very scheming look you've got there. I do not feel good about that look at all."

"This is how we'll get her back."

"By finding her dog?"

"No. By making her think we might have."

"That's cruel," Elijah said.

"That girl got me a week of detention. Everyone is still calling me Ghost Girl. Giving her a good scare is what she deserves."

Elijah didn't seem convinced, so Zee continued, "She's been bullying me since last year, Elijah. I've got to make a stand or it's never going to stop. And it's not just calling me Zero. In gym class, she knocked me to the ground twice during basketball. In the locker room, she stole my change of clothes."

"Zee, you didn't tell me any of this," Elijah said.

"Yeah, 'cause it's embarrassing, okay? I've got to show her that I'm not going to put up with it anymore. This," she said, pointing at the flyer, "is my chance."

"So what's the plan?"

"We need to lure her to the cemetery and then

we're going to give her a good scare." Zee watched Nellie turn the corner and then ripped the phone number tag off the flyer. "And I know just how to get her there."

Once the plan had been formalized, it was Elijah's job to get Nellie on board. There was no way Nellie Bloom would believe a word that Zee said to her. So while Zee slipped around the corner of the hallway near Nellie's locker—a perfect eavesdropping spot—Elijah practiced his speech and approached her.

"Hey, Nellie."

From her hiding place, Zee could see that Nellie was staring daggers at Elijah. *Don't mess this up,* she thought.

"What do you want?" Nellie asked, rummaging through her locker.

"I saw your flyers on my way to school."

"Did you find Max?"

Zee couldn't help but notice how hopeful the girl sounded.

"Yeah, I think so. He was in the cemetery. I'm almost a hundred percent sure it was him," Elijah said, leaning against the lockers.

"What color was he?"

"Black-and-gray mix, it looked like. I mean, he was a ways off."

Nellie closed her locker and eyed the boy up and down. She exhaled loudly through her nose. "Did he even answer to his name?"

"Well, no. I mean, at the time I didn't know his name. I just saw him out there and sort of whistled at him thinking he might come over. But he looked real scared."

Nellie winced. "Poor Max. I hate thinking of him sleeping outside. He must be so scared. And hungry. I know I shut the gate, but somehow he still got out. He was at the cemetery?"

"Yeah, right by the Southern Gate. I'm sure it was him."

"The new principal, Mr. Scratch, came to my house last night. We talked about Max being missing. He told me nothing mattered more than finding him. Even if I had to search every street and knock on every door. He said I shouldn't count on anyone to help me, that I had to help me. And that it was my responsibility and well . . . my fault. So I've been searching nonstop. I hung these signs everywhere. And now here you are. That must mean something, right?"

"Um, yeah. Definitely. I'm sure it was the same dog. He even had that red collar."

"If you're lying to me, Elijah," Nellie said. The look on her face meant she didn't need to finish the sentence.

"I'm not. Honest, Nellie."

"Wait, did Zera put you up to this?"

"Nope," Elijah said, though his voice went suspiciously high. "After school today. Meet me at the Southern Gate."

"I don't know where that is."

"You don't?"

"No. Normal people don't spend their time hanging out in the cemetery, okay?"

"All right, well, just meet me after school and we'll walk over together. I'll be by the buses."

"Fine," Nellie said. She turned and walked away without a goodbye. As she passed the corner where Zee was hiding, Zee could see Nellie pluck a leash from her bag and clench it tightly.

It was a simple plan. Now that Elijah had convinced Nellie that he saw Max in the cemetery, he was to bring her to the stone benches near the mausoleums and Zee would take it from there. When they met at lunch, things were going well.

"She seemed like she didn't believe me at first. But

I did a good job. I really should join the drama club. I might have missed my calling."

"You're too young to have missed your calling," Zee said.

"Not true. Don't try to stop my rise to stardom."

"So, is she going to be there?"

"I'd say our chances are pretty good."

"Perfect."

"You still think this is a good idea? I mean, you don't think this is cruel?"

"Nellie is the one who's cruel," Zee said, getting up to throw out her lunch bag. "And she wants to call me Ghost Girl? Fine, I'll give her ghosts."

Later she raided the art department's supply cabinet. Red paint? Check. Bits of tubing? Check. All she needed was the bike pump in her garage and she would be all set.

Later, after school, Zee was all set up by the time she heard Elijah's voice bouncing off the cemetery stones. The bike pump would push the red paint through the tubing she had inserted into the overgrown weeds at the headstone. She was going to make the ground bleed.

"How much farther are we going?" Nellie asked.

Zee crouched behind the tombstone, the bike pump in her hands, a giddiness in her chest. She tried not to think about what Scratch said about bullying. This was about revenge. And if anyone deserved to be pranked it was Nellie Bloom, the creator of "Ghost Girl" and bully extraordinaire.

"Just down this way. This is where I saw him."

Their shoes crunched over the stones of the pathway and then fell silent as they crossed the lawn.

"Did he seem okay?" Nellie asked, her voice high and light.

She's nervous, Zee reasoned. *Not used to graveyards.*

"Yeah, sure, he just didn't want to come to me when I called him. Like I said, I didn't know he was your dog until I saw the flyers, so I didn't know what to call him."

"He only responds to his name. He's a very—"

A deep, lone howl rose up over the ridge and hovered in the air. A spate of chills broke out on Zee's arm.

"Does . . . does that sound like Max?" Elijah asked, his voice too high, too strained. Zee could tell by the sound of his voice, just on the other side of the tombstone, that he too not only heard but felt that howl. She knew he was thinking how much it sounded like the hounds he heard at night.

"No," Nellie said in such a low whisper that Zee almost couldn't hear her. "That does not sound like Max."

And in the same moment, Zee knew it too. She knew that that long, low howl did not come from Nellie's missing dog. She knew exactly where it came from. She could still hear the question, floating in her head, clear as a bell that night. The hound stationed right outside her window. How could she be so stupid? Elijah was right; this was a terrible idea, and they all needed to get out of this cemetery as quickly as possible.

When she stood up, appearing behind the tombstone in the fading light, Nellie screamed.

Loudly.

Just the sight of another person appearing out of nowhere in the middle of a cemetery as the shadows slipped along the ground was more than Nellie could take.

Elijah tried to calm her down, and eventually she did stop. But her scream was answered by another long howl, this one much closer than the other.

"What . . . what is that?" Nellie asked, looking around. Shadows seemed to dance up out of the ground, from behind the headstones, slinking and crawling in the fading light.

How could Zee be so stupid?

Elijah and Zee exchanged a look. There was a panic in his eyes.

"We need to go," Zee said. "Now."

"What are you doing here, Zera?" Nellie said.

"This was all a terrible mistake," Zee said.

"Elijah," Nellie said, turning toward him. "What's going on? Where did you see Max?"

"Yeah, um, about that," Elijah said, looking anxious in the fading light. "We sort of . . ."

"You were lying?" Nellie said. "You didn't see Max at all, did you?"

Another howl broke the night in half. Zee's heart beat hard against her ribs, like a bird trying to free itself from an impossible cage.

"It was my idea," Zee said. "My terrible stupid idea. And now we need to go."

"Go where?" Nellie said crossing her arms.

"Anywhere," Zee said. "Your dog isn't here. It was a prank. It was my fault."

"You're the worst person I have ever met," Nellie said, stomping away before turning over her shoulder and yelling, "And you, Elijah, are the second worst."

Another howl echoed off the ridge. The chill in the air clouded Zee's breath, and she glanced up. She spotted the hounds, three of them, in silhouette at the top of the hill, their bodies black against the evening blue sky. The hunk of their shoulders, the twitch in their legs. The flick of their tails. The way they threw their heads back, all three at once, and howled.

The cry was so deep it rattled her bones. It sounded old and downright dangerous. Zee, Elijah, and Nellie all covered their ears. When the noise stopped, Zee looked back up at the ridge.

The hounds were gone.

They weren't at the top of the ridge anymore.

They were coming. She heard the thunderous pound of their feet as they charged right toward them.

"Run!" Zee screamed.

They took off in a dead heat. Arms pumping, sneakers slapping the ground, dodging and jumping over low and fallen headstones. Zee and Elijah knew this cemetery, and they both beelined for the Southern Gate. But Nellie did not. The distance between them stretched as Zee kept looking back. It was her fault the stupid girl was even here.

"Faster, Nellie!" Zee screamed over her shoulder. Elijah gave her a quick, terrified look. All she wanted was to tell him how sorry she was. How stupid this idea was. How she should have known that since the first storm, this place that used to be their playground might instead be a minefield.

Zee glanced back. Nellie was in trouble. One dog

had passed her, swung back around, and now was in front of her. Nellie was taking scared steps backward. The hound's body was low to the ground, as though it was about to pounce. A terrible growl came from its bared lips. Terrified, Nellie just stood there, crying. Zee stopped.

"What are you doing?" Elijah said.

"I've got to help her!" Zee yelled. "Just keep going."

Zee turned, heading for the nearest tree. As she bolted, she reached down and scooped up a handful of rocks from the path. She scrambled up the tree, catching and swinging her foot around the last limb just as the hound that had been chasing her reached her, its jaws snapping as it clawed at the trunk. Zee kept climbing until she was on a branch that stretched over a mausoleum. She hopped down onto the roof. She could see Nellie, stock-still and shaking. The dog was low to the ground, circling her. Zee squeezed the rock in her hand and pitched it forward with all her might, hitting the dog squarely in the flank.

It swiveled its head in her direction. From here she could see the blood running from its eyes. She tossed another rock, and this one landed right on its muzzle. The hound fled.

"Nellie, run!" Zee yelled. Zee scrambled across the branch and dropped to the ground. The hound that had been following her was also gone.

"Where did they go?" Nellie said, barely over a whisper.

"I don't know," Zee said, her eyes darting from tree to headstone to shadow. They couldn't have gone far. They were waiting. Zee could feel it.

Suddenly, Elijah came barreling toward them down the hill.

"You guys okay?" he asked, breathless. He looked all right. Muddy. Shaken. But, Zee realized with relief, still in one piece.

"We've got to get out of here," she said.

"The Southern Gate is locked. That's where I went."

Locked? The gate was never locked. "We can't go back to the Northern Gate. It's too far."

"What if that one is locked too?" Nellie asked. "Are we trapped in the cemetery? Zera, did you get us all trapped in the cemetery?" Her voice was rising in panic.

Zee needed to think. The dogs were gone, for now, but if the Southern Gate was locked, there was good reason to think the other might be. They had to find another way out. The wrought-iron gate of the cemetery was easily nine feet tall and ended in a series of unpleasant spikes. The spaces between the bars were too small to squeeze through.

"We've got to make a run for the Northern Gate. That's our only chance," Zee said. They set off at an easy trot, trying to make as little noise as possible to not draw attention to themselves. By now the sun had completely set and the shadows in the cemetery were long and lean and far too wolfish.

"Zera Puckett, if this gate is locked and we are trapped in here, you are in so much trouble," Nellie said.

"Yeah, well, maybe if you stopped messing with me all the time, I wouldn't have to do things like this."

"Me mess with you? What, like, *bully* you? That's a laugh."

"Nellie, you are on my case all the time. In gym, you hid my clothes. Then—"

"Only after you put gum on my combination lock."

"I didn't . . . well, that was only after you got me detention."

"Yeah, after you nearly broke my nose."

"Could the two of you please shut up?" Elijah said. "In case you already forgot, there are wild dogs in here. I'd like to not see them again."

"Elijah, she's—"

"Zee, now is *not* the time," Elijah interrupted.

They jogged in silence, everyone's eyes darting from shadow to shadow. Zee could just make out the edges of the Northern Gate. They were almost there.

Just a few more feet and they would be free. From behind them came a barking howl. Every hair on Zee's arm stood on end. She turned and there were the hounds, about a hundred feet behind them, waiting, their bleeding eyes staring right at them.

"Run!" Zee screamed, booking it toward the gate. The dogs gave chase. The looping, pounding thud of their paws on the ground sounded more like horse's hooves. One of the dogs leaned toward Elijah, the other toward Zee, the third toward Nellie, driving them apart.

Zee realized with sickening dread: they were hunting them.

She kept running, pulling a hard right as the dog next to her snapped its jaws. She wasn't far from the Northern Gate—if she could just keep going, she would make it to the other side. But the dog had other plans.

He came for her, claws digging into the soil only yards behind her, and she sped up as much as she could. Her chest burned from running. Her muscles felt like they were screaming at her to stop, but terror kept her moving.

In the darkness blurring around her Zee couldn't see Nellie or Elijah. There was only her and the dog, driving her forward as she dodged and swerved around tombstones. And then something terrible happened.

She tripped.

Zee lay on the ground gasping, desperate to get some air into her lungs. Where was Elijah? Where was Nellie? The cemetery was stone-cold silent. She could hear the dog snuffling around her, the crunch of dead leaves under its massive paws. It circled her, and Zee kept her hands over her head to protect herself. The muscles in her legs were coiled, ready to kick at anything that touched her. Once she could breathe again, she flipped over so she was no longer on her belly, and she saw the creature standing at arm's distance, teeth bared, lips curled back from a tangle of sharp teeth. Her fear ratcheted up her spine, filled her throat. The scream she had died in her lungs.

The dog opened its mouth, and she heard it again.

The voice, different from the howl, coming from the dog but also *not* coming from the dog. It slithered out of that muzzle like something terrible was inside.

"Hoooowww much loooooonnnggeeerrrrrr?"

Zee shut her eyes, the words slinking into her ears and filling her.

"Boys!" someone yelled in the distance. "Come here, boys! Where have you gotten off to?"

Suddenly, the dog leaped away. It let loose another earsplitting howl and took off like a bullet flying up the hill. Zee managed to turn over just in time to watch the dog dash up the hillside, joined by the other two. In the distance, she could see Elijah and Nellie, struggling to get up.

"Oh my goodness, children, are you okay?" someone yelled from the gate. It took a minute before Zee realized it was Principal Scratch. *What was he doing here?*

Elijah and Nellie joined Zee, all three of them looking dazed and disheveled as Principal Scratch came down the hillside, a tote bag on his shoulder. Zee exchanged a look with Nellie and Elijah.

"What . . . what are you doing here, Principal Scratch?" Nellie asked.

"What am I doing here? What are you three doing here?" he said. "This is not a playground. And it's a school night."

For a moment, no one spoke until Nellie said, "We were looking for my dog, sir. I searched everywhere like you said, and then Elijah here"—she dipped her head toward the boy—"thought he saw him here in the cemetery."

"But we were mistaken," Zee added. "So we'll just be going now."

She tried to walk forward, but Principal Scratch

held out a hand. With a chuckle he said, "Wait one second."

"Sir," Elijah said quietly. "We really must be going. My father will be worried."

Principal Scratch nodded and clasped his hands. "Oddly enough I too seem to be missing my dog. Well, dogs. Plural. We were just walking past the gate here and something spooked them and they just took off. The leash went right out of my hand. But," he said, shifting the tote from his shoulder, "I think you did a good job of focusing on what you wanted, Nellie."

Principal Scratch reached into the tote, which Zee realized now squirmed with something. A bundle of black-and-white fluff came out.

"Max!" she yelled as the dog darted out of Principal Scratch's hands and into her arms. She scooped him up as he licked her face. "Oh, Principal Scratch, thank you thank you thank you." Zee watched the principal clamp a firm hand on Nellie's shoulder and inhale deeply. He looked very content.

"I went to your house earlier but you weren't there, so I figured I would take him on home tonight. That said, I'm in a bit of jam myself. You three haven't seen any other dogs? Big, goofy things?"

Elijah and Zee exchanged a look. Nellie was too

busy hugging Max to care, but Zee felt something terrible stir inside her.

"What did they look like, sir?" she asked.

"Oh, there they are! BOYS!" Principal Scratch yelled, and then whistled. Up on the ridge, they could see the silhouette of three dogs. They barked and then raced down the hillside. They were shaggy and medium-sized as they crowded around Scratch and he pet them. "This is Luci, Belle, and Levi. They're a bunch of goofballs. You can pet them if you want."

Zee caught his eye when he said that, the way his grin seemed stretched far too wide. "That . . . . that's okay," she stuttered. Those weren't the same dogs that had chased them, she knew that. These dogs were smaller, cleaner, less wolfish, but something told Zee not to trust what she was seeing. Something told her there was more happening here than she understood. "We should be heading home."

They headed toward the gate. Elijah was quiet. Nellie was gushing over Max's return. But Zee kept her eyes on the principal, and he, in turn, smiled at her. It was a cold smile. A knowing smile. His dogs stood next to him, stock-still, unnervingly still. They watched her too, and something inside Zee shifted.

She did not trust Principal Scratch at all.

AT SCHOOL THE NEXT DAY. ELIJAH FOUND ZEE AT HER LOCKER. "WE
need to talk to her."

"Talk to who?" Zee said, trying but probably failing at sounding casual.

"Nellie. You know what I'm talking about.
Something weird happened in that cemetery. Those
hounds . . ." He trailed off with a shudder.

"I know that, but . . . why does she have to be a
part of it?"

"Because she is. There were three of us. There
were three hounds. It was like they picked us or something."

"Look, Elijah, if you really want to talk to Nellie

Bloom about this, I'll go with you," Zee said, shutting her locker. The bell rang as students raced through the hall to get to their classes. "But I'm telling you it's a bad idea. She's not our friend."

Zee and Elijah found Nellie at lunch.

"Hey, Nellie, can we talk to you?" Elijah said. She was at a table with her friends, all of whom turned their eyes toward Zee and Elijah. One wrinkled their nose; another snickered.

"Just for a second," Zee said through gritted teeth. She hated that Nellie, of all people, was a part of this—whatever this was. She also hated that it was *her* fault that Nellie was a part of it. If she had just left her alone, hanging up her stupid signs for her stupid dog that the stupid principal found anyway. If she had just ignored being called Ghost Girl. If she had just ignored literally everything about Nellie Bloom, then she wouldn't be in this situation.

"What do you want?" Nellie said.

"Just one second." Elijah gestured that they should move away from the table.

"Fine." Nellie paused, exchanged a look with her friends, and with a laugh said, "One. Oh! I guess time's up."

She picked her apple up off her tray and took a large bite, chewing slowly as she stared at Zee and Elijah. Zee turned to walk away, but Elijah grabbed her arm.

"We need to talk about what happened in the cemetery," he said.

"OMG," Clare Jennings, one of the girls at the table, said, "were you hanging out with Ghost Girl, Nellie? Is your hair going to turn white too?" The table fell into peals of laughter.

"Of course not!" Nellie said, a touch too loudly. "Could you imagine? I wouldn't be caught dead hanging out with these freaks. Even if that's the sort of friends they prefer."

"Look, either we're going to talk about the dogs in the cemetery last night or we're not," Elijah said. "They each picked one of us. And it means something. We need to figure this out together."

"Or not," Zee cut in. "I'm perfectly fine with it being just Elijah and me."

The rest of the girls at the table fell into silence, staring at Nellie as she nervously laughed and tried to act like she didn't know what they were talking about.

"Okay, enough, I'm done," Nellie said, trying but failing to sound casual. She got up, picked up her bag, and waltzed out of the cafeteria with Elijah hot on her heels.

"Elijah, let her go," Zee called after him. "It's not worth it."

"Yes, it is," he shot back over his shoulder. "Come on."

They followed the girl out of the cafeteria and down the hall when Nellie whirled around and whispered, "*What* do you think you're doing?"

"We're trying to talk to you," Elijah said.

"You just come waltzing up to me during lunch like that? Talking about cemeteries? What is *wrong* with the two of you? Are you ever normal?"

"Oh," Zee sneered, "did we embarrass you? Want me to go back and tell your friends about the hounds?"

"I don't know what you're talking about," Nellie said, and with a flip of her hair, she headed down the hall.

"Forget her," Zee said.

"No, she's a part of this," Elijah argued. Zee watched him run after her, a mixture of frustration and anger bubbling inside her. She didn't need Nellie. She and Elijah would figure this out on their own. What was the point of bringing Nellie into this? So she could mock them? Call her Ghost Girl? Give Elijah an even worse nickname? Zee watched Elijah catch up to her. Watched her turn and listen to him talking. She could see the anger starting to wick off of Nellie. Elijah was good like that. He knew how to calm people, set them at ease. He made sure they knew he was listening. He was the softness to Zee's hard brittle edges. Which explained why she was back here and he was up there actually getting something done. After a few more minutes, she watched Elijah stick out his hand, and slowly but surely Nellie's crossed arms unfolded. She shook his hand before casting one more scowl at Zee and heading down the hall.

"And?" Zee said when Elijah returned.

"She's on board."

"On board?" Zee snorted. "The only thing she's on board for is to make us the laughingstock of the school."

"No, she isn't. Look, regardless of what she said in front of her so-called friends, she's scared. She's just as scared as you and I are. We're all in this together, Zee. We have to fix it together."

Zee looked down at the ground. She hated all of this. "So, what did she agree to?"

"To finding out what the heck happened last night. Where those dogs came from and what it means if we're . . ."

"If we're what?" Zee said, though she wasn't sure she wanted the answer.

"If we're . . . chosen."

Zee thought about the dog's sharp fangs. The way that everything went cold, the way her whole body felt like it had been dunked in ice.

For a brief second, Zee wasn't sure she wanted to know what it all meant.

◉

When they got to Elijah's house, they were surprised to see the door was unlocked.

"Weird," he said. "My dad was supposed to work late."

Zee wondered if maybe his mom was doing better but didn't dare bring that up. She understood the way hope can turn on you, growing teeth, when it doesn't work out.

The door creaked open.

"Hello?" Elijah said tentatively. There was no answer. The foyer looked the same as always, a pair of sneakers at the door, mail on the table, the coatrack and umbrella stand. He peeked toward the kitchen. "Dad?"

But it was empty in there too. A few dishes in the sink, the fading light streaming through the windowpane over the sink. A bowl full of apples on the butcher-block table.

"Dad?"

"In here, son."

Son? Zee thought. Elijah's father never called him "son." They followed the voice into the living room and were shocked to see Elijah's father on the couch. To his right, in the other chair, was Principal Scratch. The sight of him, after last night, made Zee's stomach flip. Were they in trouble?

Elijah's father stood up, wearing a sort of dazed look. "How you doing, sport?"

When his father reached out and hugged him, Elijah instinctively took a step away.

"Dad, what's going on?"

"Mr. Scratch and I were just talking."

"Good to see you again, Elijah," Principal Scratch said. "Hello, Zee."

"Talking about what?" Elijah asked. Zee stood at the back of the room thinking about how Principal Scratch was the one who found Nellie's dog.

"About focusing on what you want. We are going to talk about your goals. There is a lot of power in thinking about yourself, Elijah," Principal Scratch said. Mr. Turner took his son's hand and closed his eyes, motioning for Elijah to do the same. But Elijah stood there, nervous and confused.

"It's okay, son," his father said. "All you need to do is think on the thing you want the most, like winning a football game, and he will help you get it."

"But, Dad, I don't play—"

"Hush, son, come." His father pulled Elijah down toward the couch. His grip on Elijah's hand looked hard and, for a brief moment, painful. "Everything you want, you can have. You just have to want it more than anything else."

Zee looked at Elijah's father, at the sort of dazed sheen in his eyes, the way they darted around the room, seeing but not really seeing. The way his hairline was matted with sweat. She looked up at Principal Scratch, who now stood over them: unimaginably tall, his dark hair, his sunglasses, his black clothes.

What was happening?

"This is really for Elijah and his father, Zee. It's best if you go home," Scratch said, looking at her. "We have work here to do. Now"—he turned to Elijah—"Elijah, you're a young person, with energy and creativity and brains. I can *feel* how creative you are. Your imagination is your greatest asset. Search your heart. Find what you want. See it happening." Scratch reached down with that red-gloved hand, the leather crackling, his grip on Elijah's shoulder firm. "Hold that picture in your mind. See it. Hear it. This is your mental rehearsal for the moment you obtain exactly what you want."

Zee made her way to the door but didn't leave. She knew Elijah was frightened. So was she. But she also knew that Scratch was doing *something*. Something that made people trust him. The way he told Abby to visualize what she wanted and then the phone rang. The way he told Nellie the same thing and then appeared with her dog. If he really could do that kind of stuff, this was her chance to find out. As she slipped toward the door, just out of their line of sight, her heart racing, she heard Scratch say, "Imagine yourself in a movie theater watching the movie of Elijah. See yourself on-screen getting what you want the most. Now get up and approach the screen. There is a door. Step inside the movie. . . ."

Zee watched Elijah, his eyes closed, Scratch's red glove gripped tightly on his shoulder, his lips moving slightly. The urge to run in there and push that glove off him, to grab his hand and get him out of there, was overwhelming.

But then she heard it, at first so faint she thought she might be imagining it, but then louder and stronger until it morphed into a voice, a high, lilting voice singing a song about a girl they called the Wild Rose. She watched Elijah lift his head as he heard it too.

"Elijah, darling, my little chicken, where are you?"

Elijah opened his eyes and with a scratchy voice said, "Mom?"

When she stuck her head out from the kitchen, her beautiful hair in those familiar springy curls, her skin shining in the warm light of the kitchen, Zee gasped. "There you are, little chicken."

Scratch took his hand off Elijah's shoulder, stepped back, pressed his hands together, and said, "Well, isn't this a lovely surprise."

"Mom!" Elijah ran to her, and she gathered him up in a hug.

Zee's breath hitched inside her. She watched Elijah, so happy, tears streaming down his face as he hugged his mother. His real live mother, there and okay and not in bed with the hiss of the dehumidifier and that vacant thousand-yard stare. Zee knew Elijah was afraid he had lost her forever and could only imagine the joy he must be feeling now. She imagined it would be how she would feel if her own mother, who she wanted so badly, suddenly appeared in her kitchen, alive and well.

But Zee's mother was gone. And just seconds ago,

Elijah's mother had been very sick. Except here she was now, hugging her son, calling him chicken and kissing his tearstained cheeks.

"Don't cry, chicken. Momma is okay. I just needed a little rest."

"Just like I told you, son," Elijah's father said. "And now she's right as rain."

Elijah's mother set a big layered cake on the table. *Where did that come from?* Zee wondered.

"What's this for?" Elijah asked.

"It's for you, darling. It's because I love you so much."

"Are you . . . okay now?" he said, glancing toward his parents' bedroom door. Just yesterday that room had been like a tomb.

"Of course, darling," his mother said, following his gaze. Her brow furrowed as she looked at the door. "There's no need to worry about any of that. I hope I didn't scare you."

She held up the knife, and suddenly the smile that a second ago seemed so warm felt like it changed. Now it seemed permanent and plastered on, and something cold stirred inside Zee. She glanced back at the door to the bedroom again, something nagging at her.

"Now, now, chicken. Your momma is all better. All better because of you. Because you wanted it and because she loves you and wants you to be happy. Right, honey?" she asked, turning to his father.

"Thanks to Principal Scratch," Elijah's father said. He wore that same strange smile.

His mother lowered the knife and slid it through the cake. "Well, that is just lovely. I've always been a big believer in knowing what you want and making it happen. Regardless of what gets in your way. We stay focused; we get ahead," she said, sliding the slice out of the cake and setting it onto a plate for him.

Elijah took the cake with shaking hands. He chanced one last look at the closed bedroom door and said, "Of course, Mom. All I wanted was this."

She bent down and kissed the top of his head. "I know you did, darling. That's why Momma is fine now."

Zee watched all of this unfold, transfixed, before her eyes met Scratch's and he smiled at her. A jagged smile. A smile cut from glass. For a second she couldn't move.

Zee glanced down the hall, at the cracked door of Elijah's parents' bedroom. She strained her eyes, and then she saw it. A figure, lying still in the bed. Then she turned, yanked open the door, and ran home.

That same night, Zee was pulled out of a dream in which she was being chased by hounds. She could hear the hard pounding of their paws behind her, could hear the huff of their breath, the clicking of their teeth as they ran after her. She awoke with a start, sitting up in bed, a panic wild and loose inside her. Realizing it was just a dream, that she was safe in her bed, that nothing was trying to gobble her up, she took a few deep breaths and then a few sips of water. She rubbed her eyes as she drank the cold water down and her focus shifted and blurred through the bubbled bottom of the water glass. She got up to refill her glass, heading to the bathroom instead of the kitchen. She told herself it was just because she was tired, not because of any chance something would be crouching in the living room.

She flipped on the bathroom light and turned the faucet to fill her glass. She watched the water fill it up and then glanced up at her reflection in the mirror.

There was something behind her.

Her breath hitched, and her heart stumbled inside her chest.

With shaking hands, she put the glass down and focused on the ghost that stood behind her in the mirror. She couldn't bring herself to turn around and look at it face-to-face. It was the same one as before, muddy face and hair, mossy green streaks along her body, hunched over like she was cold.

Zee squeezed her eyes shut, willing it to go away—*"Just please go away,"* she whispered—but when she reopened them, the ghost was still there, wide eyes staring right at her. In that moment, the ghost focused on Zee's reflection, and Zee knew that the ghost could see her too. Zee's stomach dropped, and she started to shiver. She'd never felt this cold in all her life. The room felt like an ice box. She was about to call for Abby when she remembered her sister's advice.

Just talk to her. She's confused. She's probably scared. Help her through this.

Zee squeezed her eyes shut and tried to steady her breath. She could do this. She could do this. She kept saying it until it felt possible.

When she opened her eyes, the woman was still there. She slowly turned around to face her.

"Hello?" Zee said tentatively. "Can you hear me?"

The woman turned her head, her eyes clearly fixed on Zee.

"What's your name?"

The ghost did not respond.

"I'm Zee."

The ghost opened and closed her mouth and tilted her head.

"Maybe I can help you. If you have any questions."
The ghost just stared at her.

"Do you understand me?"

"Where am I?" the ghost said softly. Her voice was scratchy and tinny like the sound of an old record. It didn't feel like it actually came from her but was instead floating about the room in circle, like an echo.

"You're in my bathroom. On Hickory Lane in Knobb's Ferry."

"I'm cold. And I want to go home," she said. "I don't know the man that was here."

"What man?"

"I don't know. He was tall and handsome. His voice was like velvet and he made these promises and now"—the ghost shivered—"I'm so very cold. I would like to go home now. Can I go home?"

"Of course you can. Do you know the way?" Zee said.

"Where's my bracelet? He said he liked it, and now I can't find it. And . . . I don't know where I am. And it's so cold and wet."

"Wet? Are you in the water?" Zee asked. "What water? What water are you in?"

"It's dark. I don't know where I am. I'm here, in the water, in the dark." The ghost started to flicker like a light going out. "It's cold."

"What is your name?" Zee said. "Maybe I can come find you."

"My name? I . . . can't remember. I want my bracelet back. I want to go home. He left me here, in these woods."

"Please, where are you? I want to help you," Zee said, a tugging sensation in her heart. She understood what Abby meant. She understood why her mother thought her gift was special. It was. She had the chance to help this woman. Now that she saw her, really saw her, she knew there was nothing to be afraid of.

"What if he comes back?" her ghost asked, her voice pinging around the room, eyes wide and fearful. "Please, I really want my bracelet back. I can't go home without it. Please."

And with that, she vanished. Zee exhaled for what felt like the first time in a long time. She waited to see if the woman would come back. Eventually Zee went back to bed, and the slow crawl of sunrise crept over Knobb's Ferry.

◉

Zee headed down the stairs the next morning, her head full of questions, her body restless from the lack of sleep. She couldn't wait to tell Abby about her talk with the ghost. But Abby wasn't banging around in the kitchen getting her breakfast together as usual. The house was eerily quiet, and as Zee headed through the dark living room toward the kitchen, she heard a faint murmur. Zee stopped cold and squinted her eyes. Was the ghost back? There was a shape on the couch. She reached over and flipped on the nearby table light. It wasn't a ghost. Instead, Abby was the small form curled up on the couch, wrapped in a blanket. She looked pale and out of it and barely glanced at Zee. She just kept talking to the phone pressed against her ear. Zee crept forward, but Abby cupped her hand over her mouth so Zee couldn't hear what she was saying.

Giving her sister some obviously needed privacy, Zee cut back into the kitchen, headed to the front door, opened it, picked up the rolled-up newspaper off the front porch, and brought it inside. She rummaged through the fridge, pulled out the milk, and got the cereal down from the cabinet. She sat down at the counter, her ear straining to hear what Abby was saying.

When her sister finally came into the kitchen, she didn't say anything. Didn't even acknowledge that Zee was there.

"Um, hello?" Zee said, startling Abby, who was looking in the fridge.

"Oh, Zee! Gosh, you scared me. I didn't see you there."

"Who were you talking to? You looked really out of it," Zee said. "New boyfriend?" Zee hoped that was the case. Abby didn't seem to have time for anything other than her, and that worried Zee.

"What? Oh, no, that was Dad."

"You were talking to *Dad*? Why didn't you let me talk to him?" Zee said, putting down her spoon. "You didn't even offer."

"I'm sorry, Zee. He had to go. But he told me to tell you he loves you."

"I can't believe you were talking to Dad and didn't tell me!" Zee said, angry that her sister was so inconsiderate. She watched Abby rummage around the kitchen, pulling out a yogurt for herself.

After a few minutes of silence, Zee added, "Well, is he okay? What is he doing? When is he going to be home?"

"He's not sure," Abby said. "He's still working."

"On what? What is he doing?"

Abby furrowed her brow and tilted her head. "Strange, I . . . can't remember."

"You were *just* talking to him."

"I know," Abby said, her gaze going to her phone on the counter beside her. She stared at it, lost in some memory before snapping out of it and saying, "Finish up your breakfast, or we're going to be late."

With that, Abby got up from the table and headed upstairs. It wasn't like Abby to be so inconsiderate, and it bothered Zee. Also, why didn't Dad demand to talk to her? Was something wrong? Would he be home soon? Tired from not sleeping and frustrated with her sister, Zee felt a small headache gather between her eyes as she pulled the rubber band off the newspaper. It fell open in front of her.

The cover story was about Deanna Jameson, the kindergarten teacher that had been missing since the storm, and Zee nearly choked on her cereal when she saw the photo.

Even without the mud and the moss and the terrible look on her face, Zee was sure of it. Deanna Jameson was her ghost.

Which meant one thing. Deanna Jameson wasn't missing. She was dead.

AT LUNCH OUTSIDE. ON THEIR BENCH. SHE FINALLY HAD A CHANCE TO talk to Elijah after a hectic day of mandatory testing. She filled him in on the conversation she had with Deanna the previous night as they watched a pack of eighth graders play a game of touch football.

"And then this morning I saw this," Zee said, unrolling the newspaper. Elijah looked from it to Zee and back again.

"And?" he asked.

"This," Zee said, tapping the image of Deanna, "is my ghost."

"Wait, the kindergarten teacher is your GHOST?"

"Shush! Could you be a little less loud, please? I've got enough problems at this school."

"Sorry," Elijah said. "It's just crazy. Should we tell the police?"

Zee scoffed. "Yeah, let's go waltz up there and tell the police that the kindergarten teacher is *dead* and I know this because she's a muddy ghost that creeps around my house."

"Yeah, I can see how that might sound weird."

"We have to find her."

"What do you mean find her?" Elijah said, lifting an eyebrow. "You don't mean like . . . *find* her, find her?"

"No, but we have to help her. She said something about her bracelet. And needing it. Maybe we can find that."

"How? We can't break into her apartment," Elijah said, looking completely freaked out, and honestly Zee didn't blame him. Last night it seemed so much easier, so much more necessary. When Deanna was in front of her, needing her help, there was nothing that she wanted more than to help this poor woman. Now, removed from that situation, in the cold light of day, it seemed harder.

Frankly, it seemed terrifying.

"But she also said she was cold and wet. If we can find the bracelet, maybe we can give it to the police and they can find her . . ." Zee didn't even want to say the next word. "It's the only way she'll rest. She'll never be at peace. She wants to get out of the water, Elijah. I'm the only one who can help her. Besides, it's . . . it's my job."

"Zee, are you sure about this?" Elijah said, balling up the tinfoil from his sandwich.

"Yes," she said with more confidence than she had. "But I don't want . . ."

"What?"

"I mean, I would rather if you . . . but if you don't want to . . ."

"Zee," he said with a laugh, "of course I'm coming with you. I mean *who* wouldn't want to? It's the stuff of Hollywood dreams."

Zee smiled and realized the only way she could feel brave about this was if she were with Elijah. "Thanks, man."

He held out a fist, and she bumped it with her own. She might not have much, but she had Elijah, and today that felt like enough.

They agreed to meet at Elijah's house after school, and they would take it from there. As she bound up the steps to his house, she felt hopeful. Hopeful that she could at least do something to help her. She wondered briefly if this was how her mother felt. Did she feel this sense of obligation? Of urgency? Thinking about her mother more and more lately felt, in a lot of ways, good, but then also bad. It was comforting to know they had this ability in common, like a thread that linked the two of them. But at the same time these were questions she would never have answers to. How hard would it be to never have an answer? At what point was she just shouting into the darkness?

Zee shook these thoughts from her head as she rapped on the hard wood of Elijah's door. When it opened, he ushered her inside.

He was giddy, the excitement bubbling out of him. "My mom," he said. "She's better."

Zee looked at him, confused. "Elijah, I was there with you. Don't you remember? Principal Scratch was here and then your mom was serving you cake."

Elijah furrowed his brow. "You were here?"

"Yes."

"Weird, I don't remember that. Anyway, come see," he said, taking her hand and pulling her into the kitchen. Standing at the counter was his mother, a mixing bowl in her hand, a dusty speck of flour on her cheek. She looked up and smiled at them.

"Well, hello, Zee," she said. "We haven't seen you in a while."

"Hello, Mrs. Turner," Zee said as they stepped into the kitchen. "Glad to see you're feeling better."

For the briefest of seconds, a confused look flickered over her face and then was replaced with that large smile. "Are you staying? I'm making cookies."

"No, Mom, we've got to go. I'll be home soon."

"Sounds wonderful, chicken." Elijah hugged his mother goodbye. As he did, Zee noticed that her smile never changed. Never faltered. It was just that same hard smile, her lips stretched, her teeth shining white. As she hugged her son, her gaze was still fixed on Zee in a way that felt *wrong*.

"Bye, Mrs. Turner," Zee said from the doorway as she turned to follow Elijah out.

"Goodbye, child." Zee glanced back once, but Elijah's mother just stood there, smiling and staring at her. She placed the mixing bowl on the counter, and Zee swore it was full of mud and stones and sticks. She shivered.

When they got outside, Zee thought about her

sister and how she needed that phone call and then it came. She thought about the way her sister was this morning, no longer able to even remember what she had been talking to their father about. The way the other night in the cemetery all Nellie wanted was her dog and then it appeared. And now Elijah's mother, here, but like Abby, strange. Something was wrong. Something was very, very wrong.

"Aren't you excited for me?" Elijah said.

"Of course," Zee said, snapping out of it and smiling at him. If she said what she was thinking, Elijah was just going to be upset. The last thing she wanted to do was take this away from him. "Of course I'm excited."

"Principal Scratch is onto something with this positive-thinking stuff. He told me to visualize her being better and it happened!"

"Yeah, and he gave me back my dog," a voice interjected.

Zee looked up to see Nellie strolling down the driveway, wearing jeans and a T-shirt, not her usual designer clothes. Zee, still on the porch, balked at the sight of her. There was a brief moment of tension.

"What are you doing here?" Zee asked.

Nellie looked around a touch annoyed, shrugged,

and said, "I'm obviously here to help figure this out."

"No way."

"Look, Zee," Elijah said, "she's a part of this. She was there in the cemetery. She was picked by those dogs just like you and I were. You can't keep pretending it doesn't mean something."

"I'm not pretending. I just don't see why we need to bring her along for *this*."

"Because, Ghost Girl," Nellie said, "Elijah told me what's going on and I actually believe you."

"You . . . *what?*"

"You heard me. I believe you. I believed you in the library too."

"Then why did you have the whole school calling me Ghost Girl?" Zee said, crossing her arms. She tried not to think about how great it felt to kick Nellie in the nose.

"Because . . . you don't make it easy for people to like you. You're stubborn and obnoxious. You talk more than you ever listen. You think you're right all the time."

"If you think for one second I care if you like me or not, Nellie Bloom . . ."

"And *yet*," Nellie continued loudly, "they do. They still like you. They hang on your every word. They listen to your stories. They think you're funny. You do basically nothing and you get everything for it."

A honking laugh spilled out of Zee. "Are you kidding? *You* have everything. You're popular and rich and your dad is famous and your parents dote on you, and—"

"My parents DO NOT dote on me, okay? You couldn't be more wrong. See, this is you thinking you know everything. You don't know anything about me."

"Well, you don't know anything about me either," Zee spat.

"Enough," Elijah said. "Fine, neither of you know a thing about each other. Here's a lovely opportunity to fix that. Can we go now?" Elijah stomped down the driveway, leaving the two girls, each fuming, behind on the porch. "Last time I checked we had a ghost to save," he called back to them.

After a beat, Nellie said, "Look, I . . . I want to help. I deserve to know what's going on. I'm a part of this now. Plus I know things. . . ."

"What kind of things?" Zee asked, but she didn't take her eyes off Elijah's back as he walked away.

"I meant what I said. That gift you have, I believe you."

Zee looked at the girl to try to figure out if she was telling the truth.

"It's not the first time I've gone looking to help a ghost."

Zee shot her a look. "What do you mean?"

"I have an aunt. She's like you. She knows things; she can *see* things. My family shamed her for it, but after what happened . . . I believed her. Also"—Nellie paused, her eyes darting around before she managed to say—"she knew your mother."

Zee froze and then whispered, "What?"

"They were friends. So it makes sense that they both had the gift. It's part of the reason my family doesn't like you. They think your mother encouraged her 'nonsense.' They're really weird like that."

"Are you two coming or what?" Elijah yelled from the end of the driveway.

Zee and Nellie looked at each other. "We don't have to be friends," Nellie said.

Zee was about to say that they were *never* going to be friends, but stopped herself because the truth was she could use another friend. Everything they were doing, what was happening to Abby, scared her to her core. The more people she had on her side the better. She looked at Nellie, and something in the girl's face softened, as if she knew what Zee was thinking.

"I'm here to help," Nellie said, a challenge in her voice. "You need it."

Zee nodded. "Let's just solve this."

She said it with a determination she didn't feel and headed down the driveway to Elijah, Nellie at her side.

The trio passed through the center of town toward the North Woods. This, Zee reasoned, was the most likely place to find Deanna's missing bracelet. Whenever she appeared, she was covered in moss and mud, and when she spoke to Zee, she talked about being in the water and being cold. There was a bog about a mile into the woods, and Zee figured there was a chance that was where the bracelet was lost. So that was where Zee was headed.

"The creek will take us right there," Zee said, standing at the lip of the forest. It was a wood she knew well, another place that she and Elijah had explored throughout their childhood. It began at the end of town, right past a playground. They hopped the chain-link fence separating the woods from the park.

"Wouldn't it be better to tell someone where we're going?" Nellie asked as they stood staring into the woods. "In case we get lost."

"We won't get lost," Elijah said. "Zee and I know what we're doing."

"Yeah, so if you don't want to come, that's fine too," Zee said, but then got quiet as Elijah shot her a look. "Just kidding," she added meekly. She didn't know why she said it to begin with. Sometimes Zee just opened her mouth and things she didn't always mean just fell out.

Zee led the way over the boulders that lined the entrance to the woods and down the steep path. As they moved farther in, so did the darkness. The thick canopy of tree branches overhead blocked out whatever bit of sunlight managed to sneak out of the cloudy sky. They followed the worn path that led to the creek, passing what was left of a small stone house. It was just the foundation and part of a chimney, but when they were younger, Elijah and Zee used to love it. Zee would make up different stories about who had lived there. Later they found strange footprints around there, marks in the mud that looked like the prints of a giant bird. From that Zee made up her first original scary story about the BirdMan, a man with bird feet that came in the night and snatched up children. He carried them off in a sack he'd tied to a stick and sold them to a witch down by the river. This was your fate if you slept with your window open. Before she told him the story, she slipped out into the woods herself and made more footprints with a stick.

She had scared Elijah so much he never wanted to come back to that little ruined stone house. It was the first time she realized how powerful words can be— how quickly the right ones can open minds, and how quickly the wrong ones can ruin a place.

The creek led them deeper into the woods, and they were quiet as they walked. The only sound was the occasional snapping of a tree branch or the crunch of leaves beneath their feet.

After several minutes, Nellie broke the silence. "Is it me or is it getting darker?"

"It's not you," Elijah said.

Nellie was right. The darkness seeped through the tree branches and slid along the ground. It nipped at their heels. Zee glanced at her watch. It was too early for it to be this dark. It was as if they'd passed through some kind of portal. Instead of the breezy, crisp October light they left behind when they entered the woods, this light felt smaller and the wind blew with more bite. This felt more like November weather, when the fall tips and tumbles down into winter.

"Maybe we should go back," Nellie said, slowing her steps. She started glancing around, peeking between the trees and over her shoulder. Zee wasn't going to tease her about being afraid because she felt it too. It was as if the woods were knitting themselves up behind them, trapping them in darkness.

But they trudged on, the trio now getting closer to each other. An especially loud tree branch snapped under Elijah's foot, and he gasped. The sound and the startle defused the tension a bit, and Zee and Nellie each slipped out a little laugh. They were being silly. It was just the woods. Zee had played here a thousand times. By the time she was in fourth grade, she could tell the difference between dangerous snakes that she had to give a wide berth to and garter snakes that were harmless. Part of the reason that she was never as scared as other kids was because of her father. He taught her to be calm, to think logically, to not let her imagination get the best of her. And so far it had worked.

Until now.

Now she couldn't shake the fact that they were looking for a ghost's bracelet. Deanna's ghost didn't scare her anymore, but the idea of what they might find in these woods did. But what choice did she have? She couldn't keep waking up at night seeing this poor woman, lost and scared, and do nothing about it. And who else could help? She felt tied to Deanna. This was the first ghost she could help. She had to get it right. She felt very strongly that it's what her mother would have wanted her to do.

The wind whipped up an especially strong breeze, and Zee zipped up her hoodie.

"What was that?" Nellie said, glancing to her left. "Did you see that?"

"What?" Elijah and Zee said in unison.

"There are . . ." The girl squinted in the dim light and then, turning pale, whispered, "*eyes*. Something is watching us!"

"Oh man," Elijah said. "What if it's those hounds?"

"We can't outrun them here," Nellie said. "Not in the dark. If those are the dogs, then we're . . ."

"So dead," Elijah answered.

"Where did you see them?" Zee whispered.

"Right there." Nellie pointed, her finger shaking. "Right between those two bigger trees."

Zee squinted and ducked her head to the left and then the right. Then she saw it! There were eyes, big ones, clearly shining even in the creeping darkness. She thought of Deanna's ghost. Could it be?

She took a step forward, and Elijah swore and grabbed her arm.

"Don't go closer! We should leave."

But Zee couldn't help herself. It was like she was pulled toward those eyes by some giant magnet. They didn't move, didn't blink, as her heart thudded in her ears. Elijah and Nellie followed her, protesting

171

that this was a terrible idea and they should go home immediately. As Zee got closer, she saw that the eyes were not, in fact, on the faces of the hounds or Deanna or any other creature. They were painted on the tree trunk, over two prominent knots.

"What the . . . ?" Zee said, reaching out to touch them. The paint was wet and came off on her fingers slippery and warm and looking far too much like blood.

"Why would someone paint eyes on the trees?" Nellie asked, wrinkling her nose. "That's just such a weird thing to do."

"That's paint, right?" Elijah said. "We're sure that's paint?"

Zee glanced around, wondering if there was someone—or something—else in the woods.

"Look!" Nellie said, pointing. "There's another!"

"And another!" Elijah added.

They spun around looking at the trees that surrounded them. All of them had eyes over the knots, all different shapes and sizes that scaled the tree trunks, climbing high into the sky. Zee spun around, dizzy, looking up at all the eyes that stared down at her.

"What is this?" Nellie said, looking around the grove. "Who would do this?"

"It's probably just a prank," Zee said, trying to keep her voice steady. "Teenagers or something. . . ." She trailed off, knowing that this was not the work of teenagers. There was something dark in these woods, something, perhaps, evil.

A shiver crawled up her spine, but before she could change her mind, she said, "We should keep going."

THEY PRESSED ON THROUGH THE WOODS. HUDDLED TOGETHER. BAT-
tling back the darkness. Nellie reached into her back
pocket and pulled out her phone.

"Guys, let's use the flashlight on our phones," Nellie said, swiping the screen. Elijah and Zee just stared
at her. "What? It'll be better with all three of us."

"We, uh . . ." Elijah trailed off, so Zee finished for
him.

"We don't have phones."

"Like at all?" Nellie asked.

"Nope."

Elijah had a phone for about six months before he
cracked the screen and his father took it away. Zee,

on the other hand, never had a phone. Her sister did, and they still had a house line. She was going to ask for one for Christmas, but then her father lost his job and that was the end of that.

"Okay, well, we can use mine," Nellie said, holding the light up. This made walking easier, but there was something about having this circle of light that threw the rest of the woods into an even deeper darkness. Now it felt like not only could they not see beyond the circle of light, but that it was some kind of beacon, summoning whatever was out there to them. Whatever had just painted those eyes on the trees could be watching them from the shadows.

"Are we still going the right way?" Nellie said, looking around nervously. "I really wish we had told someone we were in here. I don't even have a signal."

"It's not much farther," Zee said, though to be honest she wasn't even sure if that was true anymore. When they headed off the path to look at the eye trees, Zee had found it again, but the farther they walked the more she feared they found *a* path but not *the* path. She couldn't hear the creek anymore. Was she even heading in the right direction? Was the bog even this way?

The only sound was the crunching of leaves under their feet, the occasional crack of a twig, the huff of their breath, and, if one listened hard enough, the pounding of their hearts.

When the light started to flicker, Nellie tapped the screen again. Then it blinked out completely. She tried to reboot her phone, but it was dead.

"I don't understand," Nellie said. "I just charged it this morning."

As they were cast into darkness, Zee waited for her eyes to adjust. "I don't think it's your phone."

Elijah looked at her. "You think it's this place." When Zee nodded, he said, "We should get out of here right now and come up with a new plan."

Zee also wanted to leave, but she couldn't help but think about Deanna. How would she ever get free? Was she just going to spend her afterlife in this confused space, appearing in Zee's house, searching for a way to be at peace?

"I just want to go a little bit farther," Zee said. "I feel like we might be close."

Elijah and Nellie exchanged a look. After a beat, they nodded.

Now that Zee's eyes had adjusted without the light, she noticed that a steady fog seemed to have rolled through the woods. It curled between the trees as the oncoming damp settled into her bones. Her hands were freezing. She reached out for the hand of

Elijah, who in turn took Nellie's, and they made their way slowly forward. It felt like a shield, the three of them together, swallowing back their fear and moving forward into the darkening woods. There were more of those eyes on the trees here, and Zee tried her best not to look at them. They looked too real in the foggy darkness that now spread to the treetops. As they moved, it felt like the eyes moved with them. Watching.

Waiting.

The ground started to feel soft. Zee's feet sank into the mud, and she hoped they were close to the bog because that meant this was almost over. She was comforted by the feeling of Elijah's hand in hers as the fog started to get so thick she couldn't see an inch in front of her face.

"Guys?" Zee said, leading the trio through the woods. "Just stick together, okay? The last thing we need is anyone getting lost in this fog."

Neither Elijah nor Nellie answered her. Zee squeezed Elijah's hand in hers. His fingers were icy, and Zee realized they probably all should have brought gloves, though who would have thought? They certainly didn't need them before they entered the woods. It had gotten so cold that she could see her breath.

"Did you guys hear me?" she asked as they trudged forward into even spongier ground.

When they still didn't answer, Zee turned and looked back.

No one was there.

She spun around and found that there was nothing—nothing but trees and fog and darkness. Elijah and Nellie were gone.

But Zee could *still* feel a hand gripping hers.

She jumped, startled, rubbing at her palm and wondering whose hand she was just holding.

"Elijah!" she yelled. There was no answer. The woods were silent. There wasn't even the scattering sound of squirrels or deer or the flutter of an owl or a bat.

It was as if nothing lived in these woods.

A panic seized her. Where was Elijah? Where was Nellie?

"Elijah!" she yelled again. Or at least she thought she did—but with horror she realized that she couldn't hear her own voice. She tried again. And again the fog swallowed up her cries. Zee looked down at her hands, still unable to shake the feeling of that icy grip. She squeezed them together, not only to feel them but to try to stop the shaking.

A voice, low and long, rumbled across the fog.

"Zeeeeeeeeeeee."

The goose bumps raced up her arms. The voice circled her, at first on her left and then in front and then on her right and then behind her. It sounded like Elijah, but she couldn't be sure. Where was he? Where was Nellie?

"Zeeeeeeeeeeee."

For a second, it sounded like one of the hounds, and now truly afraid, Zee covered her ears to keep it out.

The urge to run was completely overwhelming. Her legs itched with the need to get as far away from this place as possible. She spun around in the fog again, her eyes desperately searching for any sign of Elijah or Nellie as her mind prayed that she didn't see anything else. The long, jagged branches of the trees stretched out of the fog like finger bones, threatening to catch her. The fog took everything, any light, any sound. The only thing it revealed were those tree eyes. They loomed and looked and mocked, peering at her from the tree trunks, still wet, still watching.

Still waiting.

Her heart thundered inside her chest, threatening to come loose. Her breathing hitched and then turned ragged and raspy. The panic clawed its way up her throat. Whatever was in these woods—and she was sure there was something terrible here—was hounding her. The fog twisted like a living thing, the cold dampness filling her lungs with every breath. Like a hand reaching inside her and squeezing her belly.

She had to get out.

Blindly, she started to run. In the dark, the trees loomed up at her. So she ran with her arms outstretched, pushing branches away from her face. Twigs broke underfoot and sounded like the snap of jaws at her heels. She couldn't figure out which way was north anymore. She was too far now from the creek. As she ran, she yelled for her friends.

Did they leave her here? Did she leave them?

Were they trapped, alone and lost in these terrible woods?

Her foot caught on a branch, and Zee went down hard with a thud that nearly knocked the air out of her lungs. She tried to steady her breathing, even as she gasped. *Calm down*, she told herself. *You have to calm down or otherwise you're going to be really lost.* She remembered her father's advice: panic is in your head. She made herself take some deep breaths like he taught her.

Inhale.

Exhale.

Inhale.

Exhale.

After she was able to breathe, she sat up, brushing the dirt and mud off her palms and knees and the front of her shirt. A few more breaths and she was just on the verge of breathing normally. With a small degree of relief, Zee noticed that the fog seemed to be lifting. She could see better, able now to make out the woods around her. When she called out for Elijah and Nellie, her voice actually carried instead of being snuffed out. Even the chill was lifting. Her arms and legs didn't feel like they were dipped in freezing water anymore.

"Zee!"

She looked back, and Nellie came charging through the grove of trees to her right. With relief, Zee could see that she looked okay, no more frazzled and panicked than Zee herself probably looked. In an unexpected move, Nellie hugged her and then helped her to her feet.

"Are you okay?" Nellie asked.

"Where's Elijah?" Zee asked. And then, feeling terrible, followed up with, "Yes, I'm . . . fine. Are you okay?"

"I'm fine. I mean . . ." Nellie glanced around the woods. "As fine as I could be. I don't know where Elijah is. I got separated from you somehow when the fog came down. I kept hearing someone calling my name, but it sounded weird."

"Like it wasn't coming from a person."

"Exactly."

"Me too. We have to find him."

They walked, side by side, calling for Elijah. It was a strange reality. If someone had told Zee yesterday that she would be here, with Nellie Bloom, she would have called them a bald-faced liar. But here she was. It didn't matter right now that Nellie said those things about Abby. It didn't matter that Zee kicked her in the nose. All that mattered was finding Elijah. And then finding their way out. That's the thing about fear: you either conquer it or succumb to it. It offers no middle ground.

They kept calling for Elijah over and over again, their voices bouncing off the trees and echoing back at them. It was a lonely call, one that offered no response but the eerie quiet of the woods. It felt devoid of all life, other than the hearts that still beat inside Zee and Nellie, and somewhere, hopefully, inside Elijah.

"What is that?" Nellie said, pointing.

Off to their right there was a small flicker of light, and then another. For a moment, Zee feared it was a forest fire, the way the light seemed to dance like only a flame can, but it was too controlled. Too small.

Gingerly they took another step toward the light source.

"Probably the same teenagers who did the eye trees," Zee said, ignoring the quiver in her voice.

"Yeah, probably. Nothing to worry about," Nellie added. Zee was struck by how thankful she was that Nellie was here. That she believed her. That Elijah was smart enough to bring her along and that she wasn't alone in these woods searching for her only friend.

Unless, maybe, now she had another.

They followed the light as it morphed and flickered, becoming increasingly clearer. They entered a break in the forest, a weirdly perfect circle of trees. On the ground there was a circle of candles burning. Zee realized this was the light she and Nellie saw from a distance. On each tree in this perfect circle hung a mirror.

And at the center of it all was Elijah.

"ELIJAH!" ZEE SHOUTED. BUT HE DIDN'T RESPOND. HE SORT OF swayed there, slack-jawed and not moving, his arms hanging at his side, his eyes locked on his reflection in the mirror across from him.

"Elijah, can you hear me? Wake up!"

He didn't move. He didn't even blink. He just stared into the mirror in front of him.

"Elijah!" Zee yelled. "Wake up."

She reached up to shake him, when Nellie yelled, "No! Don't touch him. What if it's not safe?"

"We have to help him!"

"What's he looking at?" Nellie asked. She followed Elijah's gaze to the mirrors. "We've got to knock them down," she said, approaching the mirror nearest to her. She poked and prodded, trying to tip the mirror off whatever kept it fastened to the tree. But the thing wouldn't budge.

"Here, let me," Zee said. She already had a tree branch in her hands like a baseball bat. She might not be good at much, she thought as she angled herself, but she was great at breaking things.

She swung with all her strength, and the glass shattered with a crash loud enough to hear back in town. The glass rained down, glinting against the leaves and sticks. The girls turned to avoid the shards.

"That was . . ." Nellie started but then just stood there, her mouth opening and closing.

"Look, we don't have time . . ." Zee said, but Nellie waved her hands in the air, shushing her.

"No, that was incredible."

Zee smiled, weirdly proud of herself and weirdly enjoying the fact that she had impressed Nellie. It felt good. Better than kicking her in the nose, that was for sure.

"Let me try," Nellie said, picking up another broken branch. She squared her feet and propped it up on her shoulder.

"Swing with your hips," Zee said. "It gives you more leverage."

Nellie followed her advice, nailing the next mirror with all her force. It exploded in a shatter of glass that made the girl step back, both fearful and delighted.

Zee smiled. "It feels good to break things, doesn't it?"

"You have no idea," Nellie said with a grin. "In my house . . . we don't break things. In fact, breaking things is not . . . acceptable."

Zee hefted her branch over her shoulder. "I guess it's a good thing we're not in your house, then."

Nellie smiled and turned toward the next mirror. The girls both swung with all their might, allowing cries to escape their lips, feeling the burn in their shoulders and necks as the branches made contact with the glass and it splintered under their strength. Zee thought about her teacher telling her that girls didn't behave this way, about how people expect girls to be nice and polite and small. What garbage. She was never interested in small. She was interested in the stories her mind could invent, the tales her tongue could tell, and the power her body held.

Small? she thought. *Forget small.*

Zee was going to be huge.

With that in mind, she put a touch more effort into her swing, let out a cry, and the last mirror shattered with a satisfying crash.

"That's all of them," Zee said, turning toward Elijah, hope fluttering inside her.

But the boy was unchanged. He was stock-still, his face slack and unresponsive.

"It didn't work," Zee said, looking at Nellie. "Why didn't it work?" Her voice was both angry and desperate.

"I . . . I don't know," Nellie said.

"We don't have time for this. We have to save Elijah," Zee said again, approaching the boy. She shook him this time by the shoulders, ignoring Nellie's warning.

"Wake up!" she yelled as loud as she could. What was wrong with him? Why wasn't he waking up? They had smashed all the mirrors like Nellie said, but Elijah just continued to stare into the void of space with that slack gaze. What was happening in these terrible woods?

"Maybe it's the candles," Nellie said.

Zee looked down and stomped on the first candle, which collapsed in a hiss under her boot. Nellie took out another one with a satisfying thud. Zee scraped her boot down on the next one, dragging it along the ground in a mess of wax and leaves.

For a second, nothing happened. Zee reached out a nervous hand to her friend's shoulder. "Elijah? Can you hear me?"

She shook him harder. "Wake up, Elijah!" Zee yelled, her voice bouncing off the trees and back at her.

Suddenly he collapsed, as if cut from strings, and hit the ground hard.

The girls dropped to the forest floor next to him, anxious and concerned, watching the small rise and fall of his chest.

"Elijah, please wake up," Nellie said, sounding desperate and sad. She held his hand. Zee fought back fear and something under that. Something that made her feel just a tiny bit jealous. Something that wanted to remind Nellie that Elijah was *hers*.

When he lifted his head, he blinked at them. "Zee? Nellie? What happened? There was this terrible fog, and I lost you both. Someone . . . something led me down here. I can't remember."

"It's okay," Zee said, pulling him to his feet. They brushed the leaves and dirt off his clothes.

"I don't understand," Elijah said, sounding more like himself. "I was holding your hand, and then, suddenly, I couldn't see you anymore even though you should have been right next to me. But I still could feel your hand tugging me this way."

"Same thing happened to me," Zee said.

"And me," Nellie added. "Something in these woods is trying to separate us."

"Trying to stop us," Zee added.

A cold wind whipped the leaves around them, scattering the twigs and rolling what was left of the candles. "What happened here? Is that glass?" Elijah asked.

Nellie sighed. "Yeah, you were sort of stuck in some kind of weird void that possibly had your soul trapped in a mirror universe."

"It sounds worse when you say it like that," Zee said.

"Trapped in a *mirror universe?*" Elijah said in horror as he stepped gingerly away from the glass and ruined candles.

"I think it's time to find our way home," Zee said. She wasn't giving up, but this was all too much. The eye trees, whatever tried to separate them, the fog, the darkness, and now Elijah getting trapped like that. She wanted to help Deanna, but she knew when it was time to stop and regroup.

"Elijah, did you see anyone? Do you remember anything?" Nellie asked.

"No," he said. "We were together, and then someone was calling my name. I thought it was one of you and I followed the voice down here and then the next thing I remember is you guys waking me up."

"Who would have built this?" Nellie wondered.

"Probably whoever killed Deanna Jameson," Zee said. "Probably the same person that put the eyes on the trees. They're trying to stop anyone who's looking for her. Guys, I think we need to go home."

"No," Elijah said. "We've already gotten this far."

"You could have been hurt," Zee said.

"But I wasn't. I want to go on. I want to finish this."

Zee looked at Nellie. She nodded back and said, "We've come this far. Whatever force is trying to stop us from finding Deanna's bracelet hasn't won. We can't let it."

Zee was surprised by Nellie's bravery. But then again, it seemed there were a lot of things about Nellie that Zee didn't necessarily understand or know. And also a lot of things she wished she hadn't assumed. Nellie was right. Zee did do more talking than listening, and here, in these dark woods, she promised herself that was going to change.

"Okay," she said with a nod. "Onward, then."

She stretched out her hand, making a fist, and Nellie and Elijah bumped hers.

"What we need to do first," Elijah said, "is find the

creek. That leads to the bog." He looked at the ruin around him again and shivered. "Trapped in a mirror. That's not the kind of thing you're going to forget."

Nellie breezily added, "It was nothing really. You were just, um, a little distracted."

"Yeah," Zee said with a smile. "No big deal."

"Sure. You're both a bunch of liars," Elijah said with a smile, and Zee and Nellie exchanged a small secret look. *Yes,* Zee thought, *it's time for some change.*

The trio headed back toward what they hoped was the path. They continued walking, and while the fog had lifted, they were still lost.

"There's got to be a way to figure out which way is north," Elijah said.

"Oh! I can do it!" Nellie said, excited. "I just need a stick and some sun."

"Sticks we got," Elijah said, kicking at the ground. "Not so sure about the sun."

Nellie scrounged around, picked her stick, and jammed it in the dirt so it stood upright. She brushed some leaves and twigs away to make sure the ground was level. The tree cover and clouds were not as thick here, and you could just make out a small weak shadow.

"Get me a rock," she said, not taking her eyes off the shadow. Elijah handed her a nearby stone.

"Okay, we just have to wait a few minutes," Nellie said, still watching the shadow.

Elijah caught Zee's eye. She knew that look. It was one of those aren't-you-glad-I'm-so-smart-and-brought-along-someone-who-could-help-us? looks. Normally, Zee would have smirked, but instead she said softly, "Thank you."

"What's that?" Nellie said, still staring at the shadow.

"Nothing," Zee and Elijah both answered.

Nellie placed another rock to mark the edge of the shadow now that it had moved a bit. She drew a line between them.

"Now," she said, standing, "the first rock is west and the second is east."

"Which means," Elijah said, pointing, "that would be north. Absolutely brilliant." Nellie beamed as he hugged her. "Where did you learn to do that?"

"Girl Scouts. One of the many activities my mother insisted on."

"Well, thank goodness she did," Elijah said.

"Indeed. Tennis would have been a lot less helpful," Nellie joked. "Come on, let's go."

Zee was struck with a warmth, something almost like a hug as she followed her friends. At first it was gratitude. She was thankful for Nellie's smarts and thankful for Elijah for bringing her along. But as they walked, it morphed into something else. Like a beacon that was telling her they were going in the right direction. She was warm all over. It felt like a nice protection against the cold woods.

Within a few minutes, they heard the babble of the creek next to them. Excited, they jogged down a hill toward it, relieved that the light down here felt like the warm October light. No one wanted to mention it, but it felt like they'd escaped some sort of trap, like whatever cursed that part of the woods held no sway here.

Again, the ground softened, and Zee knew they were almost there. When she was younger, this was the line that she couldn't cross. Her father let her play in the woods, but he always told her that once the ground started to sink under her feet, she had gone as far as she could. There was a lot of freedom in her household when it came to her father's rules. But this was an uncrossable line. Bogs were dangerous. It was easy to get stuck in the mud and muck. It was easy to get turned around, and even now as the ground bowed under her, she could hear her father's voice telling her it was time to come home.

Come home, Zee. Come home.

The words were whispered on the breeze, which lifted her white hair.

"Are we almost there?" Nellie asked.

"Yes," she said with confidence. Because Zee wasn't a little girl anymore. And this time it wasn't about games. She was, after all, trying to save a soul.

The trees morphed from oaks and maples to smaller shrubs. On the edge of the bog was a massive weeping willow tree, which reminded Zee of the one in the cemetery—the one she stayed away from—and she shivered even though it no longer felt November cold.

They stopped about twenty feet from the tree.

"Spread out, and be careful. The bracelet could be anywhere, but that bog is no joke," Zee said. The three of them started searching the ground, turning over leaves and kicking up dirt. After thirty minutes, it seemed they had searched everywhere but found nothing. They were tired and cold, and their boots no longer seemed to protect them from the ooze of mud.

"Maybe this is the wrong place," Nellie offered.

"Something—or someone—was trying to stop us from getting here, though. This has to be it. Didn't Deanna tell you this was the place, Zee?" Elijah said.

"Sort of. She didn't know where she was, but . . . she said it was cold and wet. This makes sense based on what she described. I just don't know."

"Yes, you do," Nellie said. "Close your eyes and think about it. You know."

"I don't." Zee felt her frustration rising.

"Zee, you have a gift. Use it. Listen for her."

Zee closed her eyes and exhaled long and deep. She listened hard, beyond the forest and beyond her own breathing. She listened with her whole body. And then she heard it. Faintly at first but a humming. A song. A song about a Wild Rose. The same song Elijah's mother was singing. And then above that she heard Deanna.

"Look up, Zee," her voice said in Zee's head. "Just look up."

Zee opened her eyes, and the voices and the song faded away. She lifted her head, gazing up into the willow tree, and spotted a glint of silver. Her breath caught. There it was. Deanna's bracelet, hanging from one of the tree branches like some kind of marker. Zee reached up and pulled it down, held it in her hands. Nellie and Elijah gathered around her, and the three looked down at the trinket in her hand. Engraved on the front was the name "Deanna." On the back it said "I will always love you."

Zee gripped it tight in her hand. "Let's go." Zee turned to go, and Elijah and Nellie followed. They didn't speak as they made their way back through the forest. This time the woods yielded to them. It was no longer as dark or threatening; the eye trees didn't appear anymore. And this time, they didn't stray from the path. And when they passed out of the woods and toward the playground, they couldn't help but notice how strongly the sun shone.

"How could it have been so dark in there?" Nellie asked as they hopped over the chain-link fence and returned to town.

"That wood felt cursed," Elijah added.

"That's because it was," Zee said.

At a pay phone, Zee slipped a quarter in and called the sheriff's station. She reported where she found the bracelet of the dead kindergarten teacher. She agreed to drop it in the mail. She did not leave her name.

That night, Deanna did not come back, and Zee hoped that the woman was somewhere peaceful. Somewhere warm and safe.

Somewhere she hoped her mother was.

15

ZEE WOKE WITH A START AGAIN AT 3:00 A.M.

The witching hour.

This time there was no storm that pulled her out of her dreams, but she still felt that nagging, clanking feeling that something was wrong. She got up and checked the window in case the hound had returned, but the streets were clear. Her water glass was empty, so she headed out to the bathroom to fill it. The house was quiet, the gentle tick of the nearby wall clock matching her steps as she padded past Abby's room. Abby's door was open. Even in the pale moonlight that shone through the window, Zee could see that her bed was empty.

"Abby?" she whispered.

When there was no answer, Zee headed down the staircase. She heard the low murmur of a voice drifting up toward her.

"Abby?"

In the living room, she found her sister, wrapped up in a blanket, her eyes staring into the distance, talking on her phone, her hand over her mouth again so that Zee could barely hear her.

"Abby?"

Her sister didn't acknowledge her, not even when she was standing directly in front of her. Zee waved and tried to get her attention, but Abby stared right through her as if she didn't exist. She thought about Nellie's advice that it could be dangerous to touch Elijah before. So carefully, Zee reached out and shook her sister's shoulder. As soon as she touched her, Abby jumped.

"Zee, you startled me," she said, still gripping the phone. Her knuckles were white.

"Who are you talking to?" Zee asked. "Is that Dad? It's late, Abby. It's three o'clock in the morning."

"Oh, I'm sorry," Abby said, looking pale and confused. She seemed smaller too, shrunk down in the blankets. "I should get to bed."

She got up and, trailing the blanket behind her,

headed toward the stairs. As she passed Zee, she said, "Dad's on the phone," and tried to hand the cell to Zee, but she missed and it clattered to the floor.

Zee watched her go shambling up the stairs, still muttering to herself. Zee waited until she heard Abby's bedroom door close.

With a trembling hand, she lifted the phone to her ear.

"Dad?"

But there was no familiar voice on the other end of the phone. No "I love you more." There was nothing but the heavy rush of static and white noise. A shushing, fuzzy noise that grew louder and louder until it hurt to listen to, until Zee couldn't stand it and, with shaking hands, she ended the call.

If there was no one on the line, who was Abby talking to? And for that matter—what was she hearing?

The next day at school, as Zee and Elijah passed through the cafeteria, they spotted Nellie at her usual table with her friends. Only this time, instead of ignoring them, Nellie got up and joined them.

"If you come sit with us," Elijah said, "you'll never be able to show your face at that table again."

"I don't care," Nellie said seriously. "We need to talk."

The trio headed outside, securing the small patch of grass where Elijah and Zee usually ate lunch. "So, what's up?" Zee asked.

"Something happened last night."

"Yeah, same," Elijah said.

"Wait, you too?" Zee added.

Zee told them about Abby on the phone and how she was talking to no one.

When she finished, Nellie said, "I woke up at three—"

"Wait," Zee interrupted, "me too."

"Also me," Elijah added. A shiver seemed to find all three of them at the same time.

"Max was gone," Nellie continued after a beat. "He usually sleeps on the bed with me, but he wasn't there. I checked the whole house, and I couldn't find him. I went out in the backyard, and the gate was open. That's how he went missing last time. So, I checked the backyard and then cut through my neighbors'. I couldn't find him anywhere."

"So, he's gone again?" Elijah asked.

"No. That's the thing. I couldn't find Max. But when I was out there, the hounds found me."

"What?" Zee and Elijah said in unison.

"All three of them were there, two in the road and one on my neighbors' lawn."

"What did you do?" Zee asked.

"I ran! I ran like a crazy person and got back into the house. My mother caught me and went into a complete meltdown like she always does if I do anything wrong. And then she told me Max was with her."

"Oh good, so he's safe," Elijah said.

Nellie shook her head. "It's not Max. I don't know how, but the dog in my house is not Max. He's mean. He growled at me and tried to bite me. Max would never do that. My Max is the sweetest thing in the world. This Max . . . I don't know. He's angry. I had to kick him out of the room, and he just paced outside my bedroom door, growling."

"That's horrible," Elijah said.

"And then, right before I fell asleep, I heard something. A voice. Asking a question."

Zee looked at Nellie. "'Howwwww much looooooooonggggggger?'"

"Yes!" Nellie said. "How did you know?"

"It's the hounds. That night I first saw the ghost, one of them was outside my house. And that's what it said."

"What does it mean?" Nellie asked.

"I don't know, but it's freaky," Zee said. She turned to Elijah. "What happened to you?"

"My mother. She was up at three a.m."

"Weird," Nellie said.

"Actually, that part isn't weird. My mother can be like that. She doesn't always sleep well, so she stays up late and bakes or cooks. Anyway, she was baking. And she asked me to get some brown sugar out of the cupboard in the hallway. So I did, and my parents' bedroom door was open, and I thought for a second that I could still see her lying in bed."

Zee's breath caught as she thought back to that day when Scratch was at Elijah's house, how she also thought she saw someone in that bedroom.

"Was she?" Nellie asked softly, as if she were afraid of the answer.

"It looked like someone was there," Elijah said. "But I figured it was just a trick of the light 'cause she was in the kitchen, I mean, I had just seen her. So, I brought the sugar out and we chatted for a bit and then . . . I saw what was in the bowl."

"What?" Nellie said.

But before Elijah could answer, Zee whispered, "Mud and sticks and stones."

Elijah just stared at her, his mouth slightly agape. "How . . . how did you know that?"

Zee closed her eyes and took a deep breath. "Because that was what I thought I saw yesterday, before we went to find Deanna's bracelet."

Elijah looked confused, but it quickly morphed into something more. Something angry. "Why didn't you tell me?"

"Because I wasn't positive, and you were so happy, and I wanted it to be true and for everything to be fixed. I wanted her to be okay."

No one spoke for a few minutes before Nellie squeezed Elijah's hand and said, "I understand why she didn't say anything, E."

E? Why was Nellie calling Elijah "E"? Zee wondered, but didn't say. Instead she said, "I'm sorry, Elijah. I just didn't want to say anything until I was sure."

"Sure of what?"

"Of this. Max being wrong. Abby talking to no one. Everything that's happened."

"And how that's not my mom."

Zee was sure she never heard him sound sadder than he did in that moment.

"Guys," Nellie said after a moment. "This is

serious. We need some kind of plan. We've got to figure out what's happening."

"No. Not what's *happening*. It's Principal Scratch. I'm sure of it. It's something he is *doing*," Elijah said with grim determination. "We need to find out what."

ZEE DIDN'T REMEMBER THE LAST TIME SHE SAW HER SISTER THIS excited for anything. Abby had been racing around the house getting ready, arguing that they mustn't be late, and then herding Zee outside, leaving half her breakfast on the counter. In the car she was humming to herself and kept weirdly fixing her hair in the mirror. Abby was acting like she had a date instead of just going to the elementary school for an assembly. This wasn't just a school assembly. The whole town was invited. There was going to be a lecture about achieving your goals. Something Principal Scratch was calling "Getting What You Want When You Want It: Putting Yourself First."

"Don't you think Principal Scratch is amazing?" Abby said.

Zee rolled her eyes. "Not especially," she said.

"But he's an actual miracle worker. It's all the customers in the diner talk about. How he came to their houses and motivated them and how the things they wanted most in life are theirs now. I just find the whole thing inspiring."

Zee turned to her sister. "Exactly what miracle has he worked, Abby?"

She laughed. "Are you kidding me? I've been talking to Dad nearly every day."

"Have you?"

"What does that mean?"

"Have you been talking to Dad? Because the other night you handed me that phone and there was no one there."

"Huh. He must have just hung up."

"No, Abby. You're talking to no one. Don't you see what that man is doing? He's got this whole town under some kind of spell! He's the furthest thing from a miracle worker that ever existed."

"I don't have time for your stories, Zee. I know exactly what Mr. Scratch has done. Look at how he's united this town. I won't have you speak badly of him."

As they pulled up to the school, there was no

parking in the lot. Nor was there street parking. They had to park all the way by the duck pond, and then, checking her watch like she'd morphed into the White Rabbit, Abby couldn't stop hurrying her sister along, yelling that they were going to be late and they weren't going to get a good seat. Zee followed, dragging her feet. She didn't want to go to school. In fact, if she never saw Scratch again, that was just fine with her.

Inside, every seat in the gymnasium was filled. Abby, unable to hide her disappointment, said, "See, I told you we needed to leave sooner."

The sisters found a spot to stand back near the doors. Zee gazed with disappointment at all the people. Looked like the whole town was here. She spotted Elijah and his father, but his mother wasn't there. She even spotted Nellie and her parents and her little brother. Nellie had her head down, and when Zee finally caught her eye, she offered a small wave. Nellie returned it. She looked about as happy to be there as Zee was.

After nearly fifteen minutes of waiting, the whole room craned their necks to watch for Principal Scratch's entrance.

He did not fail them.

Once again, adorned in his black jacket and shirt and pants, he slammed open the gymnasium doors, hair slicked back, sunglasses reflecting the light that streamed through the windows. People actually started applauding when he entered, and he bowed low when he reached the podium.

"Oh my gosh, he's amazing," Abby said. Zee looked around the room at the people gathered there and with a cold dread realized they all had something in common. Everyone looked worn and washed out. They looked tired. The only light they had was when they looked at Principal Scratch like he was their new savior. Something was wrong here. Very wrong.

"Do you love me?" the principal asked from the front of the room, his hands held wide and welcoming.

And the whole place, literally everyone except for Zee it seemed, echoed back, "Yes, we love you!"

Abby reached down and squeezed her sister's hand. She had tears in her eyes.

"Ah," Principal Scratch said, placing his hands over his heart, that red glove on the top. "That is good. I was blessed to come to this community, to meet all you lovely people, to help you realize what it was you wanted most, and to help you make that happen. I have knocked on all your doors. I have talked with you. Together we have focused and motivated each other to obtain what we want the most. Made each and every one of you into your own champions. I have watched you all speaking into existence what it is you need the most. I have watched you fight tooth and nail to make it happen. I have watched you let absolutely *nothing* stand in your way. I have watched you fight for your goals no matter the roadblocks. Over the needs of anything else. Over family and friends and the good of the rest of this fine community. I have watched you succeed!" There was a round of applause.

"You are too kind. It has been an honor, watching this community come together. Watching you all realize your potential, put together a plan for your future."

Principal Scratch strolled across the gym, his hands tucked behind his back, the heels of his feet falling loudly on the wooden floor. "But nothing has made me more proud than the turnaround this school and these children have taken." Another burst of applause rattled through the gymnasium. Abby squeezed Zee's shoulders in excitement. "This school has been transformed from a place where young girls were fighting—yes, *fighting*—into a place of learning and compassion. A safe space where your children can learn what they need to succeed. They can see it out there and just *take* it. A whole school." Here Principal Scratch frowned. "Yes, a whole school . . . except for one. The one I have failed."

The crowd went eerily quiet.

"Yes," Scratch said, hanging his head, "I have failed. I don't like to admit that, but I must tell the truth."

"No you haven't!" someone in the audience yelled, and Principal Scratch smiled sadly.

"I have. There is one among you who has not found her path. One who fights. One who fails. And her failure is my failure. Because I have not reached her, she lies. She runs through sacred spaces. She laughs in the face of her own potential. She refuses to be great."

This elicited a collective gasp.

"I know, I know. But again, this is my failure. So today I would like the chance to make this right. To help her find her path so that she can experience the same thing all of you have."

Another round of applause. Principal Scratch held his hands up to silence them. "So now I would like to invite this person to join me. So that we can all help her reach her potential. So that she can become the girl we all want her to be!"

But not the girl she is, Zee thought. Because apparently just being yourself wasn't enough anymore. Zee stared at the door wondering if anyone would notice if she left.

When Principal Scratch swung his arm out, a long dark-red-gloved finger pointed right at her. Zee thought she might faint. It had to be a mistake. This couldn't be happening.

"Yes, you, Zera Puckett. It is to *you* that I speak. It is you that I have failed. Please come, join me now, and together we will speak into existence your unending potential. We will construct the future you were meant to have."

"No, please," Zee begged. "Don't do this." Her throat was tight with tears and her breathing started to hitch and turn ragged. She looked at her sister. "Please, Abby, don't make me do this."

Her sister hugged her tight and kept telling her she loved her. For a second, Zee believed she was going to get them both out of here. They'd run as fast as they could out of this school. Heck, even out of this town. They could go upstate, find their father, and never set foot in Knobb's Ferry again. She would never have to see Principal Scratch for as long as she lived.

She tugged Abby's arm, trying to pull her toward the door, but Abby wouldn't move. Instead she looked down at her with that horribly blank face and said, "Come on, Zee. I love you. We have to make sure you are saved by Principal Scratch. We all must be saved."

Saved? Zee thought, terrified.

"Abby, please," she begged as she pulled at her sister's arm. She exchanged one frantic look with Elijah, who had his hand over his mouth, and then with Nellie, who had gone pale. Someone needed to stop this. Someone needed to help her.

"Please, no," she said out loud. "Anyone, please, help me!"

But a sea of empty blank faces stared at her. What was happening?

Principal Scratch kept pointing at her, and then, as if she couldn't stop herself, she started walking toward him. It was like a terrible magic trick. The last place she wanted to go was near this man, and yet her feet kept shuffling forward. It was like Zee couldn't stop herself as she was dragged toward this black hole of a man. Her heart hammered inside her chest, and she felt the slow crawl of one lone bead of sweat making its way down her back.

When she reached him, he smiled a cold empty smile. The way a snake, if it could, would smile at a mouse.

Abby was still in the crowd, and now it was just Zee standing in front of the incredibly, almost impossibly, tall Principal Scratch.

Suddenly she couldn't move. It felt like two invisible hands landed on her shoulders and were holding her in place. She wasn't strong enough to stop him. She wasn't strong enough to stop any of this.

With terror she realized he was going to put his hand—his terrible red-gloved hand—on her. When she felt the smooth leather clamp down on her shoulder, she nearly vomited in her mouth. She didn't want him touching her. She didn't want everyone watching this happen, but she couldn't move. *Run*, she kept telling herself, but she couldn't. She could only stand there and quiver and listen to the words coming out of Principal Scratch's mouth.

"Zee," a voice called to her, sending a shiver down her spine.

"I need all of you," Principal Scratch was saying, "to work with me. I need all of you to visualize a future for this child. One that does not involve fighting and failure. One that shows her the path. Join me, friends, to see the way."

Zee felt dizzy and confused. How did she get here? How long had she been here?

"Zee."

The voice that called her sounded familiar, like something from a dream she had a long time ago.

"I see you," Principal Scratch said. With a keen horror, Zee realized that he didn't sound like he was talking to the crowd because she could still hear that like background noise. This voice, this new Scratch voice, was *inside* her head. "I see what you want. I can taste it," he said. "Your fear tastes sweet."

Zee squeezed her eyes shut, trying to get this voice out of her head, willing herself to stand up, to get out from under his glove and to get out of the gym.

"Yes," he continued, "I see what you fear. What you are so afraid of is true. You think you were a killer from the day you were born."

And then again, faintly, someone called her name. "Zeeeee."

She opened her eyes, and before her she could see the crowd, the way they all seemed entranced as they applauded what he said. As they smiled through tears, moved by his love for this community, which Zee knew was, above all things, the most terrible lie.

"Zeeee."

Zee pulled her eyes up and scanned the gym. She could see others on the bleachers, clapping, she could see the long hardwood floor leading up to the door. A door she desperately wanted to get through.

And then she saw something else.

In the corner of the room, something flickered by the team banners. It shone bright and then faded, then reappeared, winking in and out.

"Yes, Zee, it's me."

And with a cold gasp she realized it was Deanna.

"You freed me, Zee, so now I'm going to help free

you. That man is the one that took my bracelet and left me in the water. He is not what you think he is. You must get out of here as soon as possible."

Zee's head started to swirl. Principal Scratch *killed* Deanna Jameson? It didn't seem possible. Why? Why would he kill her? She looked over at Deanna again.

"He charmed me, took my bracelet, and left me behind. He left me to die," Deanna whispered right into her ear. "Then he painted the eyes on the trees to keep watch for anyone getting close. It is a dark magic that he wields. It unleashed his powers. He cannot be beaten. You must leave at once. If you let his dark words inside you, he will start to control you. That is what he does. He has a dangerous tongue. He used me to get this position at the school. He shows people what they want, and then he feeds off them, slowly draining them."

Again she heard Scratch in her head. "This is why your father has left. Your poor sister's life has been ruined. This is what you fear the most—that you are a terrible person."

"That's not true," Zee said, squeezing her eyes, even as the tears escaped and dripped from her cheeks to the hardwood floor.

"Zee," Deanna said. "Get free and get out. Now."

Zee strained with all her might, pushing against

whatever force was keeping her frozen, with his hand clamped on her. She pulled and pushed. She felt Scratch clamp down harder, his fingers digging into her shoulder, trying to will her to stay put.

"You won't get away that easily. You must tell me the thing you want the most. Say it."

"Zee, you have to try harder," Deanna said.

She tried to push his voice out of her head, but it was no use. Scratch was stronger than her. Even as she pushed away, his voice sounded louder and closer.

There was a loud shout, a stampede of feet, and Zee was knocked to the side, free of his grip.

Elijah had tackled Principal Scratch to the ground. The crowd started to panic. Suddenly, Nellie was there too, grabbing Zee's hand and pulling her off the floor. Without a word spoken, they ran straight for the doors.

"Come back, child! You have so much potential!" Principal Scratch screamed at the top of his lungs. They didn't look back. Nellie threw open the gymnasium doors, and the three of them raced down the steps two at a time and they ran and ran and ran.

17

"GUYS. STOP." ELIJAH SAID ONCE THEY REACHED THE PLAYGROUND near the entrance to the woods. The three of them stuttered to a stop, hands on knees, breathing heavy. Zee's heart was beating hard, and the sweat that covered her body suddenly made her shiver in the cool air. She sat down on one of the swings.

She couldn't stop thinking of how easily Scratch got inside her head. How he knew her deepest fear, plucked it right out, understood it, and then used it against her. There was a hard, bitter pit inside her stomach. Something that would never be filled.

How did he get inside her head? How could he

possibly know? She never talked about these fears. Not to anyone.

A sob escaped her lips when she thought about her sister just sitting there. Abby was supposed to protect her. Was it possible that what he said was true? Did she really ruin Abby's life? Did Abby resent her because she had to drop out of school? Did her father go upstate because he couldn't look at her? Because she looked too much like her mother? Because she was the reason for her mother's death? Was that why he was gone?

And why was she the only one in town who could see what Scratch was doing?

Once they had all caught their breaths, Elijah said, "Are you okay?"

Zee nodded, wiping away the tears she only now realized were still flowing down her cheeks.

"That was terrifying," Nellie said as she suddenly grabbed Zee into a hug. Without thinking about it, Zee relaxed into her arms. Elijah wrapped his arms around the two of them, and they stood there in a little huddle for a few minutes.

"Oh my goodness," Elijah said. "I just realized I pushed my principal to the floor. I'm one hundred percent in trouble. Detention for life!"

Zee broke from the hug and looked at her friend. Was this another thing she caused? Another way she poisoned everyone around her? But when she saw the big smile on Elijah's face, she couldn't help but laugh herself. "My hero," she said.

"Nah. You don't need a hero. You're the hero, Zee."

"We'll all be heroes," Nellie said. "Once we figure out what is happening."

"Guys, I spoke with Deanna again," Zee said. "She appeared in the gym and told me who killed her." Zee took a deep breath because even saying it out loud seemed crazy. "Principal Scratch."

"What?" Elijah said at the same time that Nellie said, "No way."

"She told me that he was the one who brought her to the woods and took her bracelet."

"He must have made the eye trees," Elijah said.

"What *is* he?" Zee asked.

"I don't know, but I don't think he's human. I'm afraid he might be something worse. My aunt, the one who's like you, she warned me about this, about all kinds of things," Nellie said, "until my mother found out, and now we can't see each other. Things at home are not great."

Zee watched the look that Elijah gave Nellie as he said, "Still as bad as the other week?"

"Yeah," Nellie said, her eyes down.

A twinge of jealousy went up Zee's spine as she watched this exchange between the two of them. How much time did Elijah spend with her? Did they . . . *like* . . . each other? Zee furrowed her brow. And no, it wasn't that she liked Elijah like that either. Most days Zee wasn't sure who she liked or didn't like. Sometimes she thought that one day she might like boys. Sometimes she thought about liking girls—but not the ones at school because they were mean to her. Most of the time she liked no one and wanted to live in a castle at the edge of the sea and do nothing but write stories and own a thousand cats. But just the idea of someone else spending time with Elijah . . . made her feel, frankly, weird.

"Is there any way we can talk to her?" Elijah said. "To your aunt? Ask her questions?"

"If we can somehow get up to the New Castle library."

"Wait, she works there?" Zee asked.

"Yeah. I mentioned it like five thousand times when we were there. You don't remember?"

Zee dropped her eyes. "I maybe sort of blocked out anything that had to do with you back then."

Nellie let out a honking laugh. "Same, Ghost Girl. Same."

Zee smiled. It was amazing how words could

change over time and with experience. Something that used to feel so harsh and cruel before was now said with so much love and friendship. How experiences could change you, how people were so much more complex than you assumed.

"But how are we going to get up there?" Elijah asked. "Can Abby drive us?"

Zee cringed. She'd forgotten all about Abby. Her sister was probably so worried after she just took off like that. Then again, Zee thought, maybe she wasn't worried at all. Maybe she was so far under Scratch's spell that she didn't care about anything else.

"No, she's . . . not well. She's not herself. There's the phone thing where she thinks she's talking to Dad, but also she's just obsessed with Principal Scratch. How come you guys were able to get out from under his spell?"

Nellie and Elijah both looked nervous before Nellie said, "I don't know. The spell . . . whatever he's doing didn't latch on right. I believe Principal Scratch gave me something that looked very much like Max, but . . . he's not my dog. I don't know what he is, but he's not mine. Everything about him feels off. He's mean. He slinks around the house like he doesn't belong there. He's some kind of terrible copy. Made to look like Max, but . . . wrong."

Elijah nodded. "Same. The person in my house is . . . not my mother." There was a catch in his voice before he cleared his throat and went on. "I want it to be, so badly, but that doesn't make it true."

"We've been talking about it," Nellie said, pointing at herself and Elijah. "It was hard to come to terms with, but when you know someone . . ."

"In the same situation," Elijah added. "At some point, you need to face the truth even if it's not what you want."

Zee considered this. If Elijah and Nellie were able to counter whatever Scratch had done, why couldn't Abby? Was she that desperate for their father? Or was it all just too much for her? Zee always thought of Abby as a grown-up because she was so much older than her, but maybe twenty-one isn't that old after all. Maybe it's far too young to have to drop out of school, raise your little sister, and work yourself to the bone. Zee instantly regretted all the times she'd been so thoughtless and mean to Abby. Of course she believed it was their father. She was still kind of a kid herself.

"So," Elijah said, "how do we get to the library?"

"Easy," Nellie said. "Bus tickets."

Zee looked at her. "Yeah, sorry, I don't have money. Like at all."

"I know," Nellie said. "I do. I got all three of us."

"Won't your family notice you're gone?"

Nellie dropped her eyes. "No. They won't."

There was a beat before she added, "Zee, I'm sorry about what I said at recess before our fight. I made it all up. I was . . . mad."

"At what?" Zee asked.

"At you," Nellie said. Her voice dropped as quickly as her eyes. This was not the confident Nellie that Zee had known. There was something painful in her face. "At what you and your sister have. Everyone who goes into that diner knows she's bragging about how great and clever you are all the time. I was jealous. I don't have anyone doing that in my house. No one fawns over my grades. No one surprises me. Yes, we have money, but that doesn't fix anything. It doesn't stop people who are supposed to love you from reminding you how much you disappoint them. All I had was Max, and now I don't even have him."

Nellie and Elijah exchanged a look and something passed between them that Zee realized she would never understand. Whatever was happening between Nellie and her family was clearly akin to what Elijah was going through with his dad. Nellie was right. Zee had so much more than she realized. So much that she took for granted. She had Abby, who gave up everything to make sure she was happy, and her father, who loved her enough to trust her to take care of herself. She had Elijah, who listened to all her talking without asking for anything in return.

And now she had Nellie.

"I didn't know you could start such a great friendship by kicking someone in the nose," Zee said.

Nellie burst out laughing. "Isn't that how all the great friendships start?"

Elijah hooked an arm around both girls' shoulders. "Stop being so mushy, you two."

They met up at the bus station an hour later, tickets in hand, and boarded the next bus to New Castle. On the ride, they lined up all their facts and figures so that they had as much information as possible. They needed to get to the bottom of this.

"So what else did your aunt tell you?" Elijah asked.

"Mostly stuff about balance."

"Balance?" Zee said as they rumbled up the road.

"Sure. How the universe is balanced. The way good forces come up against evil forces."

Zee laughed, but when Nellie looked at her, she stopped. "It's true, Zee. There is evil in this world. It corrupts people, makes them harm others. It's toxic."

"Do you think Scratch has been corrupted?" Elijah asked.

"No," Nellie said after thinking about it for a minute. "I think he does the corrupting. I think he's like . . . water coming up against iron. He's the agent that does the damage."

"He's what causes the rust," Zee said, and Nellie nodded.

"Do you think your aunt will be able to help?"

"Absolutely. She's seen it all. Ghosts, hauntings, creatures that would make your skin crawl."

When the bus wheezed to a halt outside the library, the trio got off. They climbed up the wide steps and entered the library. At the front desk, Nellie asked for her aunt and was told she was at the reference desk in History and Religion on the second floor.

They took the escalator up, and Nellie spotted her right away. Nellie's aunt looked up. For a moment, she looked frozen in shock, but then she ran around from the desk and hugged Nellie as hard as she could.

"Aunt Betty, you're going to squeeze my insides out," the girl laughed.

"I'm just so happy to see you! Wait, what are you doing here? Is everything okay? Did something happen at home?" Aunt Betty said in a rush. She was so excited her curly hair full of clips and a few errant pencils bounced.

Nellie held up her hands to slow down her aunt. "Everything is fine."

Aunt Betty's squinted. "Is your . . . mother here?"

"No," Nellie said, and they watched Aunt Betty noticeably relax.

"Then what are you doing here?"

"These are my friends. Elijah and Zee," Nellie said, hooking a thumb back toward of each of them. "Zee has . . . um . . . a gift. Similar to yours."

Aunt Betty's eyes went wide, and she smiled at Zee. She ran a warm hand over Zee's head and touched the side of her face. It was a comforting touch.

"Oh my, what a powerful gift you have, Zee. You're absolutely humming with it," Aunt Betty said. "How exciting!"

Weird, Zee thought, *it's like being a part of a strange little club.*

"Wait," Aunt Betty said, and stopped. "I know you. I know this gift." She gasped then and said, "You're Laura Ann's baby."

"I told you they were friends," Nellie said.

"You knew my mother?" Zee said just above a whisper. Her voice catching on the M-word.

"I did. She was a dear friend of mine and a talented Seer. I miss her every day. You look like her."

"Everyone says I look like my father," Zee said, hardly able to control the hitch in her voice.

"You do, but you look like your mother too. You have her smile. And her talent."

"Yeah," Nellie said, "we wanted to do a little research about that."

"Do your parents know you're here?" Aunt Betty asked.

"Not really. But if they knew I was here, they'd just refuse to let me see you. You know how they are! Besides, we really need your help."

Aunt Betty fixed Nellie with a look. "Just a few hours and then you're going back home before they send the police after me, okay?"

Nellie nodded.

"What topics are you interested in?"

"Ghosts for sure. Maybe demons."

Elijah and Zee exchanged a look, and Elijah mouthed, "Demons?" He looked very anxious.

Aunt Betty exhaled deeply. "That's an intense order." She looked at Zee and said, "Have you gotten yourself mixed up in something?"

"No, ma'am. It's just research," Zee lied at the same time Nellie said, "Yes."

Aunt Betty made a face and crossed her arms. "So which one is it?"

Nellie looked at Zee and Elijah. "You can trust her. I promise."

Zee and Elijah exchanged a look and then both gave Nellie a nod. She told Aunt Betty everything. From the storm to the cemetery to Max to Elijah's mother to Principal Scratch. Hearing Nellie lay everything out like that, Zee realized how much they did need help, and she was thankful that even if she didn't know how to ask for it, Nellie did.

"So, can you help?" Nellie asked.

"Of course I can. I'm not only an expert in Seeing; I'm also a librarian!"

◉

Zee and Elijah and Nellie spent the next two hours poring over the books that Aunt Betty pulled from the paranormal section. They wrote down notes on scrap paper.

"It says in here," Elijah said, pointing at the thick tome before him, "that sometimes you can get good spirits to fight on your behalf. Do you think we could ask Deanna?"

"I could try. If what happened to her happened to me, I would want to get revenge," Zee said.

"That's what happened when my aunt helped out a ghost on Route 66," Nellie said.

"You really do know this stuff," Elijah said, giving her a warm smile.

Zee pulled a new book off the stack. She flipped through the pages and stopped when she got to a part on demons. It talked about the history of demons, but what caught her eye was a sidebar that had a list of historical names.

Azazel

Demogorgon

Hecate

Loki

Mephistopheles

It was one of the last names, a nickname according to the book, that made Zee stop.

Ol' Scratch

It couldn't be a coincidence.

Aunt Betty appeared holding a big red book, pulled out a chair, and sat down. "Kids, I think I might have found something out about this Principal Scratch." She opened the book in her hands and read from the page.

"Negative entity attachments, or NEAs, are spirits that have attached themselves to a person in order to siphon off their energy. NEAs feed off people's feelings, good and bad, as well as their ideas and imaginations. NEAs can attach to one or many people depending on their strength. They are very persuasive, and as they persuade people and drain their energy, their powers grow. If an NEA gained corporal form, it would be very dangerous."

"What's 'corporal form' mean?" Zee asked.

"It means to have a body. To have physical form," Elijah said.

"That's right," Aunt Betty said.

"So you think that Principal Scratch is an NEA?" Zee asked.

Aunt Betty exhaled slowly. "It's hard to say without having seen him do his actual work, but this sounds like what you were telling me. He starts as someone that inspires you, that convinces you that he can help. He raises people's hopes, reads their minds, their dreams, their fears . . . and then they start getting the thing they want. So they keep at it. It's a cycle, and each cycle makes him stronger. And he drains all their energy. He feeds off their needs."

"Have you ever dealt with an NEA, Aunt Betty?" Nellie asked.

"Once, but it wasn't a person. It was just a spirit."
She chewed her lip before saying, "It was very powerful, and I was much younger. Back then we didn't call
them NEAs."

"What did you call them?"

Before Aunt Betty could answer, Zee said,
"Demons."

Aunt Betty nodded. "Good instincts, Zee. When
you are tied to the spirit world, you'll see not everything is as it appears."

"Miss Betty," Zee asked.

"Aunt Betty, darling," the woman said, squeezing
Zee's hand.

Zee smiled. "Aunt Betty, is there a map of Knobb's
Ferry? And maybe some tracing paper?"

"I'll see what I can find."

After a few minutes, Aunt Betty managed to
scrounge up a map in the archive section and tracing
paper in the children's craft section and brought them
to the table. Zee spread the map out.

"Uh-oh," Elijah said. "What are we doing?"

"Just an idea I had." Zee spread the tracing paper
over the map and made a point on what would have
been her house. Then she found Elijah's and Nellie's homes and made a little dot on them. Then she
found Deanna Jameson's little apartment over the

barbershop and marked that. Then the closest she could estimate to where the bog was.

"Oh!" Nellie said, just a step ahead of Zee. "Of course."

"Why am I the only one that doesn't get what is happening here?" Elijah said, and Aunt Betty smiled at him as they watched Zee start to connect the dots.

"That's a very powerful symbol, children," Aunt Betty said, worry furrowing her brow.

"My house, your house, Nellie's house, Deanna's house, and the bog, where we found the bracelet."

"And what's in the middle?" Aunt Betty asked.

Zee marked the center with an X. "That," she said, "would be the school. At the center of this lies Scratch."

She glanced at the sidebar in the open book.

Ol' Scratch.

Zee, Nellie, and Elijah looked at Aunt Betty, who hadn't taken her eyes off the map. "You children were right to come to me for help," she said with determination.

18

"COME ON. MY CAR'S OUT BACK." AUNT BETTY SAID.

"You're coming with us?" Zee asked.

"Of course I am. I have more experience with this than you do." The trio squeezed into Aunt Betty's pickup truck, and soon they were rumbling down toward the highway.

The problem was, they couldn't get there.

"Didn't we already pass that bus station?" Elijah asked, pointing as they raced past the station.

Aunt Betty's brow furrowed. When the bus station appeared again, Zee and Nellie pointed it out.

"What is going on?" Nellie asked the third time

the bus station zipped past the truck. "Are we stuck in some kind of loop?"

Aunt Betty pulled the truck over to the side of the road. "This is some powerful magic, children. It seems the whole town of Knobb's Ferry is cursed. I can't drive you back there. I suspect no one could."

"How do we get home?"

"Oh, *you* can get home. The next bus that pulls out of that bus station will take you home. Problem is, I was going to help you. That is what that man is trying to stop." Aunt Betty pulled the truck back out onto the road, and then, when the bus station appeared again, she pulled into the parking lot. They climbed out of the pickup truck as the bus appeared in the distance.

"Come here, all of you," Aunt Betty said, hugging them all so hard they thought they were going to pop.

She looked at each of them in turn and said, "Take care of each other. Love and friendship are the strongest allies you have." She touched the side of Zee's face. "Your gift is powerful and it will help you, but you all must protect each other. And you, Elijah, watch out for them. Listen even when they cannot. Same with you, girls. Have hope, even when it seems hopeless. Let it carry you through the dark. You must believe in hope even in the dark or you shall never make it to the dawn. And most of all, hold tight to each other." Aunt Betty gathered their hands into hers. "NEAs can't feed off you if you protect each other. Keep each other clear. Don't fall prey to your wants. Or your fears. That will feed him. Don't listen to his lies. Life is full of loss. Lies do not protect us from that. Loss must be met head-on. There are few stronger ties in this world than friendship. Not even a demon can cut through that."

Nellie, Elijah, and Zee all looked at each other, grim determination set on their faces. The bus to Knobb's Ferry rumbled up to the stop. "I wish I had more time," Aunt Betty said.

"Thank you for everything," Nellie said. Aunt Betty hugged them all again, and they boarded the bus.

"Oh, and children!" Aunt Betty yelled from the sidewalk. Zee pulled down her window. "Don't forget: The trickster, no matter how powerful, *cannot* take that which is not freely given. As long as you don't give in, he has no power over you. Never forget that."

The bus pulled out, and the three of them waved frantically to Aunt Betty, knowing that now, even more than the knowledge they gained, she had given them courage.

For all of Aunt Betty's wonderful advice, the first thing she did suggest was very practical. She convinced them to get help. Since she couldn't come with them, she suggested that before they tried to confront Scratch, they needed to talk to the police. But by the time they were standing outside the station doors, that whole thing seemed insane.

"They're not going to believe us," Zee said. "It all made sense around Aunt Betty, but now it sounds crazy."

"Yeah, that's magic for you," Nellie added.

"Listen, we gave them the tip about Deanna's bracelet; that has to count for something," Elijah said. "They need to understand what happened out there in the woods and what her ghost told you about Principal Scratch. I'll even tell them about how my mother has been . . . different."

"And my dog," Nellie added.

"What if they're all under his spell?" Zee asked. "Scratch is really powerful."

"If there's any chance that we can get someone else on our side," Nellie said, "someone with authority, we should take it. And if not, we'll have to do it on our own."

Zee exhaled. "Okay, let's get this over with."

Inside the station, a bunch of police officers were milling about, having loud conversations and drinking coffee even though it was nearly 4:00 in the afternoon. None of them stopped to acknowledge the trio. Zee approached the desk. Behind it one of the police officers was seated, his back turned away from them. He was yelling to one of the other officers about the outcome of last night's game.

"Excuse me," Zee said, but the man behind the counter continued to ignore her. She had a bad feeling about this.

Nellie, clearly annoyed, banged her hand on the counter and shouted, "EXCUSE ME!"

The officer spun around and stared at the children before him. "What's that?"

"We need to talk to someone about Deanna Jameson," Nellie said. Zee was struck by how confident Nellie sounded. Nellie was a girl who demanded to be listened to.

"What was that, kiddo?" the officer said with a condescending laugh. "You want to talk about a murder? Is this for the school paper?"

This made the nearby officers laugh.

"No," Zee said, finding her courage. "It is not for the paper. *I'm* the one that called in the anonymous tip. I'm the one who found her bracelet."

He snorted in response, "Yeah, sure you did."

"I did. I found it in the bog out past the North Woods. Right along One Mile Creek."

The officer squinted. "Am I supposed to believe that you three kids found the best clue we had in this case and called it in?"

"We're not kids. We're eleven," Elijah added.

"Well, my young Sherlocks," the officer said, giving a smug smile, "how did you go about finding a bracelet in the middle of a bog deep in the woods?"

"Because her ghost came to us and told us," Nellie said. Zee appreciated Nellie including herself and Elijah. Now all three of them could get laughed out of this station instead of just her.

And laughed at they were. The officer gathered up everyone he could find nearby and filled them in. After a few more minutes of laughter, he said, "Wait. Is her ghost here now? Is she talking to you?"

Someone behind him made a creepy "ooooooohhh-hhhh" moan. Others laughed. *Amazing*, Zee thought to herself. *You never really do grow up. It's like your whole life is always going to be varying versions of school.*

"No," Zee said. "We set her free. But she told me who killed her."

The main officer shushed those around him. He

leaned over the counter, and a serious look spread across his face. Zee knew better than to trust it.

"Who? Who did she finger for the murderer?"

"Principal Scratch," Zee and Elijah and Nellie all said at the same time.

There was a stunned silence that rippled through the room before everyone in hearing distance erupted in laughter.

Zee sighed and turned to leave.

The officer held up his hands to silence everyone's laughter and said, "So you're telling me that the man who saved my marriage is a murderer?"

Someone from the back said "Yeah, the man who helped cure my son also kills pretty little kindergarten teachers?"

"And the man who got me a new home is also a stone-cold killer?" someone else yelled.

"I told you this was pointless," Zee said. They left the station, shutting the door on both the laughter and the mocking comments from those officers.

Back out on the street, Zee looked at her friends. "No one is going to believe us. The whole town is under his spell. He gives them what they want most in the world. They're loyal to him."

"So what now?" Elijah asked. "We're totally alone in this?"

Zee looked at her friends. She thought about Abby. About how washed out and wasted away she seemed. She thought about how Scratch was manipulating her, playing her like a puppet. She thought about Elijah's poor mother, sick in that bedroom while a fake one danced around his kitchen. She thought about Nellie's dog. All these people believed because of one man who was playing them like a violin.

"We were never alone," Zee said.

"No," Nellie said. "Like Aunt Betty said, we've got each other."

Zee raised her fist, and both Nellie and Elijah bumped it in solidarity. As they headed toward the school, each step felt like something was pulling them along. Something was dragging them toward it.

Something *evil*.

◉

The front doors to the school were unlocked, but the lights were out—casting what seemed familiar in an unknown light. It was just starting to get dark outside. They walked in, shoulder to shoulder, and headed down the long hallway. Zee could swear the others could hear her heart pounding. The classrooms they passed were empty.

"Where could he be?" Elijah whispered.

"I don't know," Nellie answered, "maybe visiting more families and messing with their heads."

The loudspeaker squealed to life. "Hello, children." Principal Scratch's velvety voice filled the halls and the classrooms. "I've been waiting for you three."

A shadow slid down the hall ahead of them. Was it Scratch? Zee grabbed the hand of Elijah, who then grabbed Nellie's. They watched the shadow grow closer, slinking up the wall. By the time it turned the bend, Zee's heart was in her throat and Elijah was squeezing her hand so hard she thought it might break.

Around the corner, a figure crept. But it was not Principal Scratch. Instead they watched with horror as the hound appeared in the hall, threw back its head, and howled. The cries filled the hall, and then the creature leaped forward and gave chase.

The children ran, arms pumping, for the nearest classroom, the hound close on their heels. They got inside and slammed the door shut.

"We're trapped," Elijah said, his face painted with fear. "What do we do now?"

"I have no idea," Nellie answered.

After a few minutes of pacing and barking and scratching at the door, the dog started to whine before it gave up and trotted down the hall.

"Do you think it's gone?" Zee asked as she took a

few tentative steps toward the door. Nellie and Elijah followed as the trio cracked the door open and peered down the hall. It was empty. The hound, it seemed, had been scared off.

There was a loud crash behind them as desks went flying. All three of them screamed at once. Zee spun around. The hound was *inside* the classroom. Zee stared with horror at the open window. She didn't even have a chance to tell them to run before they were charging out of the room. The creature was hot on their heels. They all turned right at the next hall, sprinting down to the science wing and the cafeteria. Before they could reach another classroom, another hound appeared ahead of them.

"This way!" Nellie yelled, pulling them toward the gymnasium. They yanked the doors open and tumbled inside, then shut them again just as the hounds slammed up against the wood. Zee, Elijah, and Nellie scrambled backward into the darkness of the gymnasium. Elijah got up and found the big light panel on the wall. He flipped the switch up.

Principal Scratch stood in the middle of the room.

Nellie reached for Zee's and Elijah's hands.

"Hello, children. Are you finally ready to confess?"

"We don't believe your lies," Nellie said, just like

her aunt had told them. "You can't hurt us because we know what you are."

Principal Scratch threw back his head and laughed. Outside the doors he was answered by a lone howl. Then another.

He strode toward them. The trio scurried away as he approached and shot out that one red-gloved hand and snapped his fingers. A surge of heat, like electricity, sizzled through their hands. Nellie hissed and let go.

"Did you really think that would work on me?" Principal Scratch asked with a smile. "Do you not know who I am?"

He flexed that gloved hand out again, and they froze in place.

Literally.

Zee couldn't move her legs anymore. She couldn't move her arms. She managed a side glance toward Nellie and Elijah and saw that they were also stuck fast.

Oh no, she thought. *What have I done?*

Principal Scratch took his time walking toward them, each click of his boots on the shiny gym floor tapping a terrifying tempo. He hooked a finger under Zee's chin and lifted her head up. His sunglasses slipped down his nose just enough for Zee to see his eyes. She squeezed her own shut. But it was too late. If she survived this, she would never forget what they looked like. Stone-cold black eyes—no white, no iris—just endless black with red pupils. Like two perfect drops of blood floating in the dark.

"What are you?" Zee managed to ask.

"I am your nightmares. I am your doubt. I am your weakness and fear and jealousy. I am everything you hate about yourself. I am hate itself. And I have been walking with you your whole life."

He stood in front of them. "I know what you yearn for. I can see into your hearts. All of you," he said, holding his hands out.

"You," he said, pointing to Elijah. "I have fixed your mother."

"That *thing* is not my mother," Elijah growled.

Principal Scratch ignored him, "And you. I saved your little dog. Don't you see? I give and I give and I give. I have healed this town. And, in exchange, I only get one small thing."

"What?" Elijah asked.

"Nourishment. Fulfillment. Each wish is a morsel. Each desperate want, a bite. You see, when they talk to me, I get to feast on their souls. Bite by bite, I eat them up, until there's nothing left. I'm almost done with some of them. Soon they will drop to the ground, nothing left but a worn-out husk. They're all so deep into their fantasies they can't even see themselves wasting away. So determined to get what they want, they don't realize what's happening. Humankind is weak. They will abandon each other for their own desires. Eventually you three, who have proved so difficult to manage, will give in too. And I will relish eating your wishes and hopes and dreams. So young. So fresh. So tasty."

Scratch stretched that red-gloved hand out toward them as if he could pull their souls right out of their bodies.

19

PRINCIPAL SCRATCH STOOD BEFORE THEM. HIS RED-GLOVED HAND extended like a weapon. "My children have chosen you. They have deemed you special and for that I will do anything. I have already given you so much. But I am a generous man. I can give even more."

He extended a hand toward the gymnasium door. Through it came a familiar little bark and Zee and Elijah looked at Nellie. The mini poodle ran down the aisle, whipping past Scratch. He jumped up toward Nellie, and she scooped him up in her arms. *Wait,* Zee thought. *A few seconds ago, Nellie's arms wouldn't even work. Now she's holding Max. If that even is Max?* He licked Nellie's face and whimpered a scared little cry before leaping down and wiggling on the floor.

"Yes," Scratch said, standing behind Nellie. "I can give so much more." He held his arms out like he was being bathed in a warm light.

Like he was being fed.

"Nellie, no!" Zee yelled. "That's not Max! You have to fight him. That's not your dog."

Nellie looked up at Scratch with a dazed look on her face. Almost as if she had never seen him before in her whole life.

"Nellie, fight him!" Elijah cried. When she turned to look at him, she offered up the same blank expression that Zee had seen on the other people in town. Scratch clamped a firm tight hand on the back of the girl's neck.

We're losing her, Zee thought with fear. "Nellie, let him go! That's not Max!" she yelled. Zee tried to move, to get to Nellie, but she was still paralyzed by Scratch's power. "You have to get out from under his hand!"

Nellie turned toward them and smiled a smile that did not reach her eyes. "It's Max!" she said. "My good boy."

"Nellie, please!" Zee cried.

Scratch released his hand from Nellie's shoulder, and she swayed for a brief second before going slack.

Max, at her side, shifted and grew. His hair turned from black-and-white to tawny and rough. As Zee watched, unable to move, unable to scream, he transformed into one of the hounds and howled a cry Zee felt in her bones.

Scratch stepped back from her, and Nellie swayed there, still upright, but limp and vacant and so far from okay. It reminded Zee of the way Elijah was in the woods. *What was going to happen to Nellie?* Zee wondered. How were they going to help her?

At the back of the gymnasium, a figure appeared. Zee squinted trying to make out who it was. Could it be someone that will help them? The police? Another teacher?

As it moved closer, Zee's heart leaped into her throat. The blurry figure morphed and changed shape, an outline against the gym walls, running toward Elijah.

"Oh, chicken!" the figure called.

Zee watched Elijah's breath catch as his mother ran right up to him. "We were so worried when you didn't come home. Thank goodness I found you."

She bent down on her knees in front of him. "Are you okay, sweetheart? Where have you been? Your father and I were so worried." She looked around. "What are you doing here?"

When she leaned up to hug him, Zee watched Elijah relax into her arms, the warmth of her, the familiar smell, the thud of her heart. She kissed his head.

"Would you like to go home, darling?"

"Yes," he answered sounding exhausted. "More than anything."

"Elijah!" Zee yelled. But the boy just gave her a blank look, like he'd never seen her before. Scratch already had his hand clamped on Elijah's shoulder, but all Elijah was focused on was the fake mother before him.

"Elijah, please," Zee sobbed, the tears running down her face. "I know you think that's your mother, but it isn't her. Please! It's Scratch making you see what you want to see. Remember what Aunt Betty said!"

"Zee?" Elijah said weakly. "I feel so strange."

"You have to fight him, Elijah. Please. I can't lose you!" Zee glanced frantically at Nellie, who remained unchanged, the hound circling her swaying body.

"Look at me, chicken," Elijah's mother said, turning his face back toward hers. "I missed you so much."

A sob broke out of Elijah. "I thought you were gone. I thought you were never going to get better."

"Elijah, please!" Zee yelled. Her voice hitched as she cried. "Please don't give in. Your mother is still at home and she's still sick and I know that's scary but it's true. This is not your real mother."

"But, it is," Elijah said as his mother kissed his cheek. "She's better now. All I wanted was for her to get better and she is."

"You've got to let her go." Fat tears rolled down Zee's face. She knew how hard it was to accept the awful truth. She knew how scared Elijah was, how much he wanted this. Scratch's cruelty hit her like a punch in the gut.

"But she's better," Elijah said as the tears slipped slowly down his cheek. "If she's better, I don't have to lose her again. You don't understand."

"I know what it's like to lose someone," Zee said, her voice hitching. "I know how scary it is, but, Elijah, please, I'm begging you. That is not your mother. Your mother is at home and she needs you."

"Lil' chicken," his mother whispered in his ear. "You know that it's me. I'm so sorry for scaring you. I'm sorry for getting sick. But I'm better now. The doctor came and helped me. Things are going to change, I promise."

"Elijah, please! You have to fight it," Zee sobbed next to him. "Get out from underneath him!"

"I'll take you home now, chicken. Just me and you."

Elijah nodded, but his face twisted. "I don't feel good."

"Elijah," Zee begged, "fight back!"

"I promise never to get sick again. I know you were scared and I'm so sorry, but we've got each other now." She touched his cheek, brushing away a tear. "You want to come with me?" She stood and reached out a hand. "I'll take you home now."

Zee watched with horror as Elijah's head started to slump forward and his eyes rolled back in his head. Scratch was draining him. Soon, he would just be an empty thing like Nellie was.

"Elijah, you have to fight him! Please!" Zee cried. "You have to stay with me so we can save Nellie." When he turned his head and she could see him focus on her, her heart lifted. "Yes, that's it. See me. I'm right here. I'm real. She isn't real, Elijah."

He looked back at his mother, who still stood before him with her hand outstretched.

"Let's go home now, Elijah," his mother said, pulling on his hand. "I'll make you a cake."

He looked up at her. "A cake?"

"I'll make you a cake of sticks and stones and dried-up leaves." Her face stretched in a wide, wicked smile.

"What did you say?" Elijah asked in a shaky voice.

Her smiled stretched longer, like her chin was extending; her eyes shone a touch too bright. "I know it's your favorite."

"No, please no," he sobbed.

Suddenly, Elijah gasped and pulled himself out from underneath Scratch's hand as the thing pretending to be his mother cried out. She hunched over, her arms and legs contorting, and then sprouting fur. She landed on all fours, her face growing long and lean, a snout full of jutting fangs. The cry now turned into a howl.

"Hoooowww muuuchhh loooonnnnnggggeeeer?"

Zee watched Elijah's body suddenly fill with life. His head lifted and his eyes opened as he gasped for air.

"That's it, Elijah—fight him!" she yelled. He looked dazed and ashen, but he wasn't as far gone as Nellie. Elijah somehow managed to get out from under Scratch's hold, and whatever that thing was that was pretending to be his mother had crept away.

"Boy, you are proving to be quite a nuisance," Principal Scratch said. He flexed his hand, and Elijah landed with a thud on the floor. Zee called for him, but he didn't stand up.

Zee started to yell for someone, anyone. "Help!"

she screamed. "Someone help us, please!"

Suddenly the gym doors flew open and her father came charging in. "Zee, baby, are you okay? What's going on here? Who is this man?"

"Dad!" Her breath caught.

"Darling, come here. Get away from that man."

"Dad, please help me!"

"Baby, it's me," her father said. "I just got home. I've missed you and Abby so much. Look, she's here."

Behind him, Abby came running through the gym. "Zee, I'm so sorry about before. I didn't realize what I was doing. I was just confused. I'm not sure how it even happened."

Abby and her father both ran to her and hugged her. She collapsed into their arms. They felt warm and real. They were here to save her.

There was a pressure on the back of her neck, and suddenly it felt like her shoulders were on fire.

Then a voice in her head, a voice that sounded a lot like Elijah, said, *No one can save you but yourself.*

Her father grabbed her hand and pulled her away from Scratch. He held her tight, and the burning feeling was gone.

He was here. This was real.

"Zee, sweetheart," her father said, holding her

face between his palms. They were so warm, and her cheeks felt so cold.

"Are you really here?" She looked around for Principal Scratch, but she couldn't see him. Her father must have scared him away. That must have been what happened.

"Yes, baby, we're really here and we love you."

"We love you, Zee," Abby said. "I hope you forgive us."

They each took one of her hands and walked her through the gym toward the open doors. She passed Elijah, still on the ground. Was he in pain? What was he yelling at her? Fight back? Against who? Everything seemed fuzzy. She glanced back. There was Nellie playing with Max. Look how happy she looked. She had everything she wanted.

In the background, she could hear Elijah yelling her name, but it sounded like it came from a tin can on the end of a string. Why was he telling her that this wasn't her father? Why was he begging her not to leave him alone? He told her to remember what Aunt Betty said. Why did that feel familiar?

Have hope, even when it seems hopeless. Let it carry you through the dark.

Something was wrong. Zee knew it deep down in

her belly. She was forgetting something. Something very important. Something she told Nellie to remember. Something she told Elijah to fight. Aunt Betty told them to take care of each other. She glanced at him again, the way he stretched out his hand to her, the way he cried. Was that really Elijah?

He cannot take that which is not freely given.

But what did that even mean?

"Zee," Abby said, pulling Zee's eyes away from her friend. "Please tell us you forgive us."

"Of course," Zee croaked, "I love you both."

Abby hugged her tighter. "Good, because we forgive you too."

"For what?" Zee said. Her head hurt. Something was wrong. Abby looked *strange*. Sort of dead-eyed and blank. Zee looked at her father, and he looked the same.

"Darling," her father said, lifting her chin. "We forgive you for what you did to your mother."

20

"W-W-W-WHAT?" ZEE STAMMERED.

"Fight them, Zee!" Elijah yelled. It sounded like he was crying. "Keep your head clear! Scratch is messing with your mind. You're seeing things that aren't there."

Zee looked at her father. She steeled her voice. "You're not him. You're not my real father."

"Abby," her father said, "help me. We must get her out of here. I don't know what that man did, but we must protect her." Her father pulled hard on her wrist.

"No," Zee yelled, pulling back. "You're not my father."

A look of anger passed over his face, contorting it. "Of course I am, you little murderer. I'm your father and this is your sister."

"No," she said. And then she screamed with all her might as she pulled herself away from them. As she did, the fake version of her father and sister vanished in a wisp of smoke.

She was free! She could move. Zee ran across the gym toward Elijah, who was pulling himself to his feet. "Look," Elijah said, and pointed at Nellie up by the bleachers. She was still in a catatonic state, staring blankly at the hound that was circling her.

There was a low growl from behind them. At the doors, hackles raised, were the other two hounds. Zee and Elijah scurried away from them but toward Scratch. He raised a hand, and the doors to the gym slammed shut.

As the dogs passed, Zee heard the voice once again, asking that question it had always been asking. A question Zee was sure she didn't want the answer to.

"Hooooowwwww muuuuccchhhh looooonnnn-gggeeerrrr?"

"It is time, my lovelies," Principal Scratch said, reaching out to the hounds. Elijah and Zee moved back against the wall to avoid the dogs that trotted across the gym, but they didn't even seem interested.

They only cared about Scratch. They gathered at his feet, sitting too still, too un-doglike, and Zee and Elijah stared in horror.

Speaking to the hounds, he said, "My children. You have suffered for too long in these bodies. You have chosen new forms."

The hound next to the catatonic Nellie howled in response.

"They marked you back in the cemetery," Scratch said, pointing at Zee and Elijah. "Get out, while you still can."

"No," Elijah said. "Not without Nellie."

"You will get no other warning," Scratch said, lifting his red-gloved hand, and the gym doors banged open as if offering salvation.

Zee thought about all the things her father had taught her. How to stand up for herself. How to stand up to bullies, even if those bullies were adults. She thought about what Aunt Betty had said, about how they must hold tight to one another. About how consent was their weapon. Or maybe, their shield.

That which is not freely given.

And then Zee Puckett threw back her head and laughed.

"No," she said. "That's not how it works. You can't threaten us."

"You don't know what I can do," Scratch said, his voice velvet smooth. It carried through the gym and landed all soft and whispery in her ear. It was somehow worse that he didn't yell.

She stood her ground. "You can't just *take* our dreams, our hopes, our souls."

"I won't give you this opportunity again. Get out."

"Zee," Elijah whispered, "what are you doing?"

"I'm calling his bluff. It's just like Aunt Betty said," Zee whispered back. And then to Scratch she said, "You can only take what is given to you freely. You show people what they want the most. When they believe your lies and whatever you conjure up, they offer up their hopes and dreams and you eat them little by little. But ours are not freely given. Not even you, Scratch, can take what was not offered. *That* is the pact in all the stories. For centuries, that has always been the rule."

He looked angry, but he made no move to defy her. He tilted his chin up and said, "Are you so sure of that, little girl?"

"I am. If there's one thing I know, it's stories."

Scratch watched them for a beat and then laughed low and long. "Shame. You both would have made fine homes for my children. And I so wanted to eat every morsel of your dreams. Especially yours, Zera."

He strode over to Nellie, and the hounds followed him. "So be it. Stay, then. Watch your friend fall lifeless."

"No!" Elijah yelled. "Nellie, wake up!"

But Nellie stayed where she was, looking like an empty doll. A doll that was ready to be filled with something else.

With a snarl, the hound that was with Nellie knocked her to the ground, pinning her down. It pulled its head up in a howl and then opened its jaws. The hound's mouth stretched wider and wider than should have been possible, unhinging like a snake. From its distorted mouth came the question, "Hoooooowwwwwwww muuuuccccchhhhh looooooonnnnnnggggggeeerrrr?"

Scratch yelled, "You have waited long enough. Now is the time!"

The hound reared up on its back legs, its huge paws in the air above Nellie. Out of its wide twisted mouth came a stream of black smoke. It was a dark, deep blackness, the blackest black, twisting like a tornado up to the roof of the gym, before dropping down and heading toward an unfazed Nellie.

"Yes," Scratch said. "She is yours now."

"NOOOOOO!" Elijah screamed, and ran forward. He sprinted across the gym, Zee on his heels.

He shoved the dog aside. The shaggy body fell over and vanished in a thick pile of black ash.

Scratch yelled and dived toward him, but Elijah was fast. Before the smoke could reach Nellie, he'd already pushed her out of the way. Everything slowed down to stretched seconds as Zee realized what was happening.

"No," she whispered, running toward Elijah, but it was too late. "No, no, no, no!"

The thick tornado of smoke missed Nellie.

But it found Elijah.

Zee stuttered to a stop, her heart hammering as she watched the smoke fill her friend. It tunneled into his mouth, wrapping itself around his head. Elijah stood there, arms thrown out, locked in place.

"Elijah! NO!"

He collapsed to the floor as the last little wisp of smoke disappeared down this throat.

In a panic, Zee turned Elijah over and looked at him.

No. No. No. No, Zee thought. Not Elijah. She couldn't lose him. She laid her head on his heart and heard the small pitter-patter of its beats. He was still alive.

But was he still Elijah?

"Elijah, wake up," she said, gently shaking him.

Please wake up. Please. She begged with her voice, and her mind, and her heart. Why hadn't it been her? Why hadn't she beaten him here? "Elijah, wake up, please!"

She shook him again, harder. His eyes fluttered. She could see movement behind his lids.

"Yes, Elijah. Come on. You're going to be okay."

His eyes fluttered open and looked right at her. Zee gasped and scurried away.

They were all black with a bloodred pupil.

"No," Zee whispered, her back against the bleachers. She pulled her legs up against her and cried. This was all her fault. She was supposed to stay home after the storm. If they had not been in the cemetery, the hound would never have found her. If she hadn't been so determined to prank Nellie, the hounds would never have found any of them.

If it weren't for her, Elijah would be okay. If it weren't for her, her sister would be in college. Her mother would be alive.

All those times she'd read *Frankenstein* she'd always thought that she was the doctor—the creator, the one who brought things to life, the one who made something out of nothing—but now she realized that wasn't true.

I am the monster, Zee thought.

"My son," Scratch said, and Zee watched in horror as Elijah stumbled to life, taking awkward shaking steps toward him. He was almost at Scratch when Elijah collapsed to his hands and knees.

"Rise, my child," Scratch said. "Rise and enjoy your new body."

A few feet away, Nellie woke from her stupor. "Elijah? Zee?"

Zee covered her ears. She couldn't bear to hear her own name.

Elijah—or what used to be Elijah—rocked slightly on his hands and knees. His breath hitched.

"That's it, my child. Stand up. For too long have you walked like a hound. Stand."

But Elijah didn't stand. Instead he started to pitch forward, violently. His body was racked with great shuddering spasms, and then, with a cry, he turned and exhaled a long stream of black smoke out of his mouth.

Zee sat up, wiping at her tears. Could it be?

The smoke poured from him for what seemed like forever. Scratch screamed and clawed at the air as the smoke vanished.

When the last tendrils leaked out, Elijah coughed and sat up. He looked directly at Scratch and with a ragged but determined voice, a voice that sounded much older than his eleven years, said, "That which is not freely given."

Scratch fell to his knees, cursing. The two remaining hounds howled in grief.

Elijah looked at Zee. With incredible relief, she saw that his eyes were normal. She ran to him. "Are you okay?"

He nodded and with a raspy voice said, "That was *weird*."

He hiccupped, and a last puff of black smoke came out.

Zee laughed and then wiped at her tears again. Nellie appeared at his side. "Guys, what just happened?" she asked. "The last thing I remember was coming in here."

"We'll catch you up later," Zee said, turning toward Scratch.

He was up on his feet again, hovering over them. He was furious. He stretched that red-gloved hand toward them and Zee put her arms out, protecting her friends.

"NO!" she yelled. "That which is not freely given."

"How *dare* you?" he hollered.

"You take and you take and you take. You convince people that they want something and that want matters more than anything. But you're wrong. What matters is taking care of each other. What matters is being there for each other. What matters is friendship. And that is something you can never ever have."

There was a terrible sound like a freight train screaming, and the doors to the gym blew open. Zee hung on to her friends. They couldn't hear each other over the noise. But they could see Scratch.

Before their eyes, he shifted, his jaw split open. Dark smoke tunneled out of him as his body dropped to the floor, a pile of ash.

The smoke that was once Principal Scratch swirled through the air, and all three of them covered their mouths, fearful that he, like the hounds, would pick a new home. It swirled and dipped around the gymnasium like a terrible dark ghost.

The hounds also turned to ash, their bodies rising into one giant tunnel of smoke blasting straight out the gym doors.

Zec and Elijah and Nellie ran after it. The smoke raced through the halls and out of the school, swirling up into the sky before dipping and heading straight for the ground. It streaked toward the school lawn and smashed into the dirt and vanished. For a second, everything was still.

Then a ripple washed over the ground like the whole earth was shaking.

And then nothing.

"Did we . . . ?" Nellie asked.

"Did we just . . . ?" Elijah trailed off.

"Yeah," Zee sighed. She smiled at her friends. "We just won."

◉

When Zee returned home, she found Abby at the kitchen table.

"Oh my gosh, there you are!" she said, gathering Zee in a hug. "Are you okay? What happened?"

Zee wasn't sure where to start. She noticed that Abby looked less wan. She had color in her cheeks, her hair didn't look so damp, her eyes no longer puffy.

"What is it, Zee?" Abby asked.

"What's the last thing you remember?"

Abby exhaled her eyes searching the room. "Your principal was here. He wanted me to focus, to visualize what I wanted. And then my phone rang. Everything after that is a little fuzzy."

Zee's lip quivered, but she kept the tears in. "Everything is okay now," she said, hugging Abby. "I love you so much."

"I love you more."

"I love you *both* more," said a voice from the doorway.

Zee spun around, and there he was. Her father, his dusty work boots on his feet, his hazel eyes, his bearded face, standing in the doorway. He looked older. Weary. For a second, she paused. "Is this real? Is it really you?"

"Of course it's me," her father said. "I couldn't get ahold of you guys, not on your cell or the house phone or even at the diner. Everywhere I called I got a busy signal. So, I panicked. Came right home. Drove through the night. It was the strangest thing, though. It was like one night lasted for weeks. No matter how fast I drove, the road just stretched on forever. Like something was keeping me away."

Zee let a little sob escape her lips and ran to him. He held her while she cried, her heart drumming out a thankful beat.

Whatever had happened in Knobb's Ferry was over. Whoever, *whatever*, Scratch was, he was gone now. He had lost. The terror that the storm had dredged up so many nights ago had finally cleared.

And most important, Zee had her family back.

ZEE MET NELLIE AT THE END OF THE DRIVEWAY. SHE LOOKED NER-
vous, as if she was in a place where she didn't belong.

"Nice flowers," Zee said.

"Thanks," Nellie offered quietly, shifting the bou-
quet to her other hand.

"There's nothing to be nervous about," Zee said.

"I'm not." Nellie cleared her throat. "Are we going
or what?"

"Sure."

Zee bounded up the steps and rapped hard on the
door.

Elijah opened the door and smiled. "Hey," he said.

"Hey yourself," Zee said, punching him in the shoulder.

Then he turned toward Nellie and pulled her into a hug. "I'm so glad you came," he said. "Come inside."

"Thanks for, um, inviting me," Nellie said nervously.

Zee watched them and rolled her eyes. Is this what happened when you liked someone? Did you suddenly act so weird?

Elijah ushered them into the living room. On the couch sat Mrs. Turner. She was slender and petite, and her hair was in pretty box braids down her back. She had a smooth beautiful face and bright laughing eyes. She radiated a warmth that felt like sunshine.

"Zee," she said, standing and folding her into a hug. "And you must be Nellie."

"Yes, ma'am," Nellie said.

Elijah's mother laughed. "No need for all that formality."

Nellie relaxed into her smile, and Zee could see the nervousness wicking off her. "These are for you," she said, holding the flowers out. "Thank you for having me."

"Well, aren't you the sweetest? Thank you. I'll go put these in water. Dinner should be ready soon. We're having ham and macaroni and cheese," she said, pausing. "Not that bread crumb–topped kind, though." She glanced back and smiled. "The béchamel-topped kind." She disappeared into the kitchen but then popped her head back out. "Nellie dear, my lil' chicken has been saying the *nicest* things about you." She winked at Nellie, and Nellie smiled.

"Mom!" Elijah said, blushing. "Stop!"

"I don't tell lies, Elijah Watson Turner," she laughed, and disappeared again.

"'Chicken'?" Nellie said with a smile.

"Don't you start too."

"How's your mom doing, Elijah?" Zee asked.

"When we got home, after, you know, *that* night, she was up but weak. She seemed out of it, kind of confused. But that happens with her. My dad found her a new doctor, and he diagnosed her as bipolar."

"What does that mean?" Nellie asked.

"It means she has depressed days, where she doesn't want to get out of bed or do anything. Then she has manic days, where she'll bake all day and do everything. Then she has days where she's balanced. He gave her some medication to make the sad days less sad and the manic days less manic. It's early still, but I think we're finding our way."

"How's everything with your dad?" Zee said.

Elijah shrugged. "About the same. He's trying, though. He even asked about my advanced classes and how things were going. I don't think he fully understood what I was talking about but . . . he's trying. And he stopped talking about sports and exercising so much. I appreciate that."

"That's great."

"Speaking of that night . . ." Nellie said, "I found Max! I got home, and as I was climbing the porch steps, I heard whimpering. He was under the front porch. Poor thing looked like he'd been through . . . well, you know. But he's okay now."

"It's really Max?" Zee asked.

"Yes," Nellie said with a little laugh. "It's definitely the real Max."

"You should have brought him," Elijah said.

"I didn't want to assume."

"Tomorrow, how about I come by and we can take him for a walk? I'd like to meet this infamous dog," Elijah said.

Nellie smiled. "That sounds great. Zee, you should come too."

Mrs. Turner stuck her head back into the living room. "Dinnertime, kids."

The ham on the table glistened, and the macaroni and cheese was all crusty and golden brown.

"Oh, Mrs. Turner, this looks amazing," Nellie said.

"That's because it is," Elijah said.

"But save room for pie, dear," his mother added.

They gathered round the table, bathed in the warm light of the kitchen, the laughter of Elijah's mother, and a gentle tune that played over the stereo.

"We should pray," Elijah's mother said, and everyone clasped hands.

Nellie and Zee and Elijah exchanged a nervous glance. After everything, Zee didn't know what to pray for. In fact, she kind of had everything she wanted in that moment. She thought about Principal Scratch and how he made people focus on what they *wanted*. She thought about the way it all got distorted when people did that. When they put their desires before everything. The way they got corrupted.

So instead of praying for something she wanted, she sent a little gratitude out into the world.

Gratitude, for good friends.

◉

The following evening, the sun was just starting to set when Zee slipped on her boots.

"Where you going, hon?" her father asked from the living room.

"Just for a walk."

"To Elijah's?"

"No. There's someone else I want to see."

"You know I trust you, but don't be long, okay? Dinner's at seven."

"I'll be here, I promise."

Zee headed through town, taking her time. It wasn't that she had to work up the courage, it was more that she wanted to be ready. Things at school had gone right back to normal. There was no record of Principal Scratch, and no one seemed to remember him. It was like the whole town had woken up from some long, sleepy, strange dream.

Zee smiled to herself. One day she would write *that* story down.

She wended around the headstones until she reached the gates of the new section. She thought about how this was where it had all started. This was where she had seen the first hound.

But tonight, the shadows held no danger.

Her first stop was a shiny new headstone. The name engraved there made her smile a small sad smile. She hadn't heard from Deanna since she'd helped Zee get away from Scratch at the town assembly. Zee took comfort in this knowing that she had done it—she had helped Deanna find peace. Like a breath held too long, finally exhaled. "Safe travels, Deanna. I'm glad you're free."

Then she turned toward the willow tree, took a deep breath, and pushed the gate open. This part of the cemetery was neater, the headstones in more even rows. In the light of the setting sun, it was actually peaceful.

She knew where to go even though she'd never been there before. It was only a few rows ahead, tucked back from the road over a little hillside. She sat down in front of the stone. Traced out the letters cut into the rock.

LAURA ANN PUCKETT
BELOVED MOTHER AND WIFE
FOREVER MISSED

She thought it would be hard to see the date, her own birthday carved in that stone, but it wasn't. It was sad, but she felt like she could finally stop running from it. Like she could finally be forgiven.

Or more so, she could forgive herself.

"Hi, Mom," she whispered, "sorry it took me so long to get here."

Zee sat on the ground, her back against the headstone. She picked at the grass. And she talked to her mom. Some things she could say out loud. Others were too hard, so instead she said them in her head and hoped they got to where they were supposed to go.

When the shadows stretched, she got up, traced a finger across the stone, and headed toward the gate. She looked back once when she reached the willow tree, and stopped.

It was faint, just a flutter of light and dark, an outline mostly, but still clear enough to not be a trick of light.

Zee raised her hand and waved.

"I love you," Zee whispered. "I'll come see you again soon."

There was a rush of warm air suddenly. Too warm this far into fall. But it was real and it wrapped itself around her like a hug. It was the same as the warmth she felt in the woods when they were looking for Deanna's bracelet. Zee smiled, realizing it had been her mother there with her in the dark and dangerous woods.

Maybe she had always been there.

Zee headed out through the gate, letting the willow leaves touch her shoulders as she passed them by.

She had promised her father that she wouldn't be out late.

And, as the story goes, Zee Delilah Puckett wasn't the type to break a promise.

ACKNOWLEDGMENTS

A small loud-mouthed towheaded little girl named Zee has lived with me for close to ten years, popping up in occasional short stories insistent that she get her own tale. So here you are, Zee. I'm sorry it took me so long.

It seems impossible to account for everyone whose input large and small had a place in these pages, but I'm going to try and do my best.

So many wonderful people helped bring this book into existence, but first and foremost, thank you to my incredibly generous agent Rena Rossner, who loved this book from the beginning. Rena, you have always believed in my writing and my storytelling and you've been with me on this journey from day one. I couldn't have had a better agent, partner, and friend at my side.

Next time you're in town, drinks are on me.

Thanks to my extraordinary editor, Sara Schonfeld, who championed this book from the start. You took the time to meet with me and talk about this book's potential and how to make it even better, and that made me realize that you were the kind of editor I dreamed of. You worked tirelessly with me, all the while honoring my writing and the story I wanted to tell. Thank you for bringing Zee and Elijah and Nellie's story to life with compassion. Everyone at Katherine Tegen Books has been amazing to work with, especially Katherine herself, who helped steer this story in the right direction. Your insight and help was invaluable. Thank you to Laura Harshberger and Mark Rifkin, the managing editors; David DeWitt and Joel Tippie and the rest of the design crew; Kimberly Stella and Vanessa Nuttry and everyone in production. Thank you to Jacqueline Hornberger and Jessica Gould for your wonderful copy editing and proofreading. Thank you to Bill Wadman. And thank you especially to Maike Plenzke, whose art brought Zee and Elijah and Nellie to full beautiful color. This little book is so lucky to have such an incredible team to help her fly.

But it wouldn't be a book without my amazing beta readers. Thank you to Jes Oliveri, Greg Andree,

Amber McBride, and especially Tomi Tsunoda, who helped me see what this story was really about. You all have my deepest gratitude. And I cannot thank Rob Berg and Jeremy Voss enough for YEARS worth of writing help and support. You both stopped me from tossing my manuscript off the pier at Sixty-Eighth Street. For that, I am grateful.

To all my Renegades, especially Amber McBride, Linda Epstein, and Kath Rothschild—I am so lucky to be a part of this wild little gang. Flame Chickens and avocados and goats forever. You make Twitter a joyful space. One of these days we'll all get to Highlights.

None of this would have been possible if all those many years ago a small magazine had not taken a chance on me and published my first short story. So to Jersey Devil Press—especially Eirik Gumeny, Monica Rodriguez, Laura Garrison, Sam Snoek-Brown, and Mike Sweeney—thank you for giving this girl a shot and for all the support over the years. You made me believe I could tell a story that people would want to read. That simple act put me on the road to making my dreams come true.

To my Ride or Dies—Tomi Tsunoda, Jes Oliveri, Beren Weil, and Cindy Lutz-Spidle—it is an absolute joy to know you wonderful women all these years later. Drama Club friendships never quit. You know that I love you all and from the bottom of my heart thank you for your friendship and your constant support. Here's to another forty years.

And my other Ride or Dies—Natiba Guy-Clement and Julia Pelaez—thank you for giving me a reason to come to that library every day. You guys are the best. Your support through this—and everything else—is unmatched. And remember, we ride at dawn.

I would be remiss if I didn't thank the music of Nick Cave and the Bad Seeds—a band I pretended to be into for years (I know . . .) but whose music found me at the exact right moment. When the thunder crashed on a track called "Tupelo," I found a ghost story and Zee found a home. So, thanks, Nick.

Thank you to the Vernola family—you all filled my childhood with so much love. But none more than you, Dan. I couldn't have asked for a more magical person to grow up with. From the woods, to the Bird-Man to the Eye Trees, to the courts, to the rock, to listening to all my stories, to Fanteris—we made magic out of sticks and stones. You are my best friend and you have my heart. You will always be my Peter Pan.

Thank you to the Grochalskis, who have supported and cheered me on from day one. I love you all.

And thank you to my amazing sisters, Stephanie

and Jennifer, and their families, especially my nieces and nephews—Nick, Neve, Annie, and Wesley—who continue to teach me how beautiful life is.

Thank you to Big Ron and Trish the Dish, my mom and dad. Thank you for, well, everything. Thank you for my amazing childhood and for all the trips to the "big" library in Newburgh. Thanks for reading that first short story I wrote when I was eight and encouraging me to keep going. Thank you for always supporting this dream of mine. You were my first champions and for that I am eternally grateful. I love you more.

And finally, to my amazing husband, Jay. None of this would have been possible without your continued love and support. You helped me laugh through all the tears and you believed in me when I couldn't believe in myself. You made this dream come true. There is no one I would rather walk this wild amazing beautiful path with. Till the wheels come off, my love. And remember . . . I'll wait for you and should I fall behind, wait for me.